# the White
# WICKER
# CHAIR

Short stories by
MARCIA ELIZABETH ROSE

# the White
# WICKER
# CHAIR

Short stories by
MARCIA ELIZABETH ROSE

**MEREO**
Cirencester

# Mereo Books

1A The Wool Market Dyer Street Cirencester Gloucestershire GL7 2PR
An imprint of Memoirs Publishing www.mereobooks.com

The White Wicker Chair: 978-1-86151-670-1

First published in Great Britain in 2016
by Mereo Books, an imprint of Memoirs Publishing

The address for Memoirs Publishing Group Limited can be found at
www.memoirspublishing.com

The Memoirs Publishing Group Ltd Reg. No. 7834348

The Memoirs Publishing Group supports both The Forest Stewardship Council® (FSC®) and the PEFC® leading international forest-certification organisations. Our books carrying both the FSC label and the PEFC® and are printed on FSC®-certified paper. FSC® is the only
forest-certification scheme supported by the leading environmental organisations including Greenpeace. Our paper procurement policy can be found at
www.memoirspublishing.com/environment

Typeset in 12/18pt Plantin
by Wiltshire Associates Publisher Services Ltd. Printed and bound in Great Britain
by Printondemand-Worldwide, Peterborough PE2 6XD

# CONTENTS

# First love

———❦———

As David gazed across the crowded room, he suddenly found himself looking at a woman he had never thought he would see again. He would never forget those beautiful green eyes. It seemed to him that they were the only two people in the room; everyone else had faded into the background. For a few seconds, it seemed as if time itself stood still.

Could it really be Kerry, after all these years? Was it possible? Yet he knew even while he was thinking these thoughts that it was her; he would never forget those eyes.

He started slowly to walk towards her, but just then a waiter came up to offer him a drink from a tray, and he turned from her gaze to decline it. He looked back, and in that brief moment, she was gone. In a panic he started looking for her, but she had disappeared as if by magic.

He decided to seek out Shirley, the woman she had been talking to, and see if she knew where Kerry had gone. Shirley told him Kerry had had to leave because she felt unwell. She told him Kerry was married to the painter whose works they were celebrating this evening.

At this point, a man came up to Shirley and said "Where did Kerry go?" He seemed very annoyed. Shirley explained that Kerry was unwell, that she had gone back to rest and she would not be joining them for the rest of the evening

"I'll just go and check that she is all right, then I'll come back" said the man. He sounded annoyed, rather than concerned.

Just as he was about to leave, a young blonde woman came towards him. "Andre, how wonderful to see you again!" she said. "Please show me your wonderful collection. I insist on a personal tour."

"Of course, madame" said Andre, and duly escorted her to his collection. It appeared to David that he had forgotten all about his sick wife.

Kerry, meanwhile, could not believe that she had just seen David. He had not changed at all; there were a few streaks of grey hair, but that only made him look more distinguished. She thought her heart was going to burst. She could not believe it was really him after all these years.

As she saw him walking towards her she was in such a panic that she ran from the room into the lift to go to her bedroom. She was shaking so much she could hardly put the key card in the door. She felt sick. She hoped her husband had not seen her reaction, because she knew that if he had seen her talking to another man he would not only punish her, he would destroy David if he saw them together. She quickly texted Andre to say that her shoulder was very painful and that she was going to have a hot bath, take some painkillers and go to sleep and that she would see him in the morning.

It was ten years before this that David had left university, where he was studying to be a doctor. He had met Kerry at university. She was his first love and he was hers, and they were soon inseparable. She was also training to be a doctor, but before commencing her career, she wanted to take a year off to see Paris. Kerry loved Paris and the arts and she wanted to try her hand at painting before returning to London.

They continued to keep in touch, regularly writing to each other, but after eight months the letters from Kerry had stopped. Eventually he had a letter from her saying she was very sorry but she would not be writing to him again in the future, because she was now married, and she hoped David would forgive her and find someone else.

David was heartbroken. He could not believe it. They had originally agreed that after her year in France she would return and they would get married. He had had no hint of this from her previous letters.

David continued to look at the paintings, but he now decided that he must find Kerry. The lady had said they were staying at the hotel where the exhibition was being held, so he decided on the spur on the moment to try and find her room number.

He left the exhibition and managed to find a flower stall that was still open. He bought a bunch of red roses and returned to the hotel. At the reception desk he said he had to deliver them to Mrs Kerry du Pre. The receptionist offered to take the flowers to the room, but David said his boss had insisted he deliver them personally. Reluctantly the receptionist gave him Kerry's room number.

On his way up to her room David was feeling emotional. How would Kerry react? Would she be angry with him for seeking her out? After all, she was a married woman. But he knew that he would not rest until he had spoken with her.

He very gently knocked on the door. After what seemed an eternity, a quiet voice said "Who is it?"

"Room service" said David. "I have a delivery of flowers for you, madame."

Very slowly Kerry opened the door. She was overwhelmed to see David standing there with the most beautiful bouquet of red roses. She could not believe he had found her. She could not speak for a moment.

David gently stepped into the room. As she turned away from him, David saw that she had a large black bruise on her shoulder. He asked what had happened.

"I'm always bumping into things," she said. "I fell as I slipped on some water after my shower this morning. It will soon get better, I'm sure".

They talked for hours, although it seemed like minutes. Eventually, after many tears, Kerry told David her story.

She had arrived in Paris on a beautiful sunny day. All along the road people were displaying their works of arts. Kerry loved it there and she got chatting to a lady who was selling some pictures. Kerry bought one of her paintings and carried on admiring the other works of art.

When Kerry had met Andre, she had found him to be handsome and quite a charmer. He had invited her out to dinner, and as it was her first day in Paris, she agreed to go if she could bring her friend with her - she was staying at her friend's house in Paris for the year. Andre was very popular. Everybody liked him, and they spent more and more time together. Eventually he had asked Kerry to move in with him. She had only been in Paris six months, but she knew she was starting to fall in love with him.

A few months later Andre proposed, and she accepted. As soon as she said yes, he opened a bottle of champagne to celebrate. Then he ushered her into a taxi and whisked her off to a little church in a very small village. She was overcome with excitement.

Andre said that he wanted to show her the church where he wanted them to get married, but inside the church, Kerry was surprised to see the little chapel alight with candles and to be greeted by the vicar. Andre had arranged for them to get married there and then.

Kerry was dizzy. She'd been drinking champagne to celebrate her engagement, and now she was getting married!

"But I'm not dressed" she said. "And what about my friends and family?"

But Andre insisted, so she agreed, and the ceremony went ahead. They spent a honeymoon touring France in a rented car, feeling blissfully happy. When they arrived back at their small apartment, Kerry rang to tell her parents. They were shocked, but at the same time they were pleased that Kerry was so happy. She promised them that she would bring Andre to meet them later in the year.

Then Andre decided that they needed to move to a better apartment. They could afford it, he said, as his paintings were selling so well now. They rented a lovely apartment with a view of the Paris skyline.

But during the move, Andre found David's love letters to Kerry. He was furious that she had not told him about her earlier relationship, and made her write to David to end it. He then threw all David's letters into the fire. Kerry was very upset, but she told herself that Andre was only jealous because he loved her so much. That was when she wrote David her last letter.

Kerry joined an art class and became a very good painter herself. One afternoon, after she had finished a painting, she put it on an easel in Andre's studio to dry. He was having an exhibition the next day. After it had dried, she placed a dust sheet over the painting and put it to the back of the room.

On the day of the exhibition, she decided to go shopping so that she would not be in the way of Andre's customers. Many people came, but only one person bought a painting. Late in the afternoon, however, a gentleman asked about the painting under the dust sheet. He asked Andre how much he was selling it for.

Andre was taken by surprise. He mumbled dismissively "Whatever you think it's worth". The man said he would be prepared to pay 300 euros, and asked if Andre had more paintings like this for sale.

Meanwhile Kerry was having a lovely day strolling around the markets. She had bought some lovely hot fresh bread, some cheese, grapes and a bottle of wine for them to have after the exhibition had finished. She returned home just as the last customer had left, without buying anything. As she walked through the door Andre screamed at her about her painting. She had never seen him so angry. He threw her basket on the floor. The bottle of wine shattered and the contents were all over the floor, but what shocked Kerry most was the change in Andre. When she went to pick up her shopping from the floor, he kicked her in the face and walked out of the apartment, calling her a traitor. Kerry was horrified. What on earth had happened?

On his return, Andre explained about the painting and said that she had humiliated him. How dare she put her work up in his exhibition? But the real reason for his anger was that her painting had sold for a greater amount than any of his.

That was the first time Andre had hit Kerry, but unfortunately it was not to be the last. He made her give up painting. He said there was only room for one artist in their household, and that was him. He changed so much that Kerry hardly recognised the man she had married.

Andre's paintings started to sell, but slowly. Eventually, desperate for income, he told Kerry to start painting again. She loved painting, as it was her escape. She painted some beautiful scenes of Paris, and Andre took them and sold them.

After a few years of this, he bought a small studio to display her many paintings and became very important in the community. He never wanted Kerry to come to the studio, so she stayed home in the apartment painting or just sitting on the promenade, happily painting what she saw. She did not mind at all, as here she was happy. Eventually their relationship improved and Kerry became pregnant. Andre was ecstatic and treated her like a princess, while Kerry felt that she had her Andre back.

But then one evening Andre went out with friends to celebrate the news of the pregnancy. He came home very drunk, to find Kerry asleep in bed. He woke her up and asked her to make him a drink. Kerry was very sleepy and said "Andre, it is so late and I am so tired, can you not make yourself a drink tonight?" Furious at this rejection, Andre dragged her out of bed and kicked her in the stomach. Then he went out.

Kerry was in dreadful pain and was bleeding heavily, but she managed to call for an ambulance. She left a message on Andre's mobile phone to call her. She did not remember anything after being lifted in to the ambulance.

The next day Andre heard the phone message and came to visit her in the hospital. He found her still unconscious. He told the staff that he had been away on business and said that Kerry had called him and told him that she had had a fall, so he had come as soon as he could. The doctors said that the severe bruising on Kerry's stomach from the fall had resulted in her having a miscarriage.

When Kerry woke up from her operation she was devastated at losing her baby, and even more devastated when she was told that she had been given a hysterectomy. She decided that she would have to start thinking about leaving Andre.

For a few months after her operation Andre was full of remorse and guilt. Then one afternoon he told her it was her fault that she had lost their baby. If she had only listened to him this would not have happened!

Kerry could not believe that he now blamed her for losing their child, when it was his abuse that had got them into this situation. It was then that she realised that she could not live with him any more, and asked him for a divorce. Andre agreed that they would live separate lives, but said he would not divorce her because he said his career would suffer, as a few people really liked her paintings.

Over the next few years, Kerry continued to paint. Painting was the only thing that kept her sane. Andre never hit her again; he was too busy having affairs to be concerned with Kerry. He now lived over his studio.

One day Kerry was feeling very lonely, so she decided to go to the studio shop as she had not been inside it before. She looked around the gallery. It was beautiful decorated, but nearly all the paintings were hers, while only a few were Andre's. What shocked her even more was the price tag on her paintings. None of them were under 1,000 euros, and some even had SOLD stickers on.

The blonde girl who was serving at the counter asked her if she could help, and Kerry decided to ask about the paintings.

"They are beautiful aren't they? Andre is such a talented painter," said the girl.

At this point, Andre came out wearing his white shirt. Kerry noticed that it had splashes of paint on it, obviously to give the appearance that he was busy painting in the studio. In fact they were just for show, to suggest to his customers that he was still the great painter. Ever the showman, Kerry thought.

Andre was shocked to see Kerry and motioned her to the back of the studio. Kerry again requested a divorce, and Andre again refused. However he did agree that he would give her half of the money for the paintings if she would agree not to divorce him and to keep on painting. Kerry agreed, as she had no money of her own. She felt trapped, but she realised on reflection that her life was not that bad really. She had the apartment, which she had decorated to make her own, and she had her paintings to keep her busy. The extra money she would get from Andre would be used to save for the day when she would eventually leave him.

A few years later, Andre visited her with the exciting news that the Waldorf Hotel in London wanted to exhibit his paintings for their French week. The invitation was for Andre and his wife to stay at the hotel free of charge with all their expenses paid. Then during the week, they would put on an exhibition of a selection of his painting which were for sale.

Andre was so pleased that his work was being recognised in London. He asked Kerry to accompany him on the trip, and she agreed. They arrived at the hotel the day before to set up the exhibition, then retired to their adjoining bedrooms.

The exhibition was very successful, but after three days, Kerry bought up the subject of the divorce again. Andre was furious. How dare she do this to him just as they were about to go down to the exhibition? He was so angry that he lashed out at her and she banged her shoulder on the wall. He said "You are my property, bought and paid for, and you will never leave me. I am Andre the famous French painter and you will obey my commands. I expect you to be at the exhibit on time at 6 pm. You will conduct yourself in a proper manner and there must be no hint whatsoever that we are not happily married, otherwise you know what the consequences will be. This is the most important exhibition of my life and you will not ruin it for me. Do you understand?"

Kerry nodded and he left the room. She then

locked the adjoining bedroom door and wept.

It was that evening, when she eventually managed to go down to the exhibition, that David saw her for the first time in ten years.

As David listened intently to her story, he was amazed that Kerry had managed to stay with this man for so long. He then told her that she had to get out of her marriage. She replied that she had already packed all her things before she had left Paris. She had all the money that Andre had given her for the paintings, as well as her passport and all her personal jewellery. She told David that she was prepared to give Andre one last chance, and then ask for a divorce. If he was not willing to divorce her, she was planning to stay on in London after the exhibition had finished.

It was then that David told her she could come and live with him in his apartment until she felt stronger and had recovered from her fall. He said he could take her suitcase for her now, and all she had to do was leave the hotel in the morning with her hand luggage.

Kerry felt sad that her marriage had to end in this way, but she knew Andre would never change. She asked David if his wife would mind having an ex-girlfriend staying with them, to which he replied that he had no wife. He said that although he had dated many women, he had not fallen in love with any of them. He then gave Kerry his card with his address and phone number on.

When it was time for David to leave, they agreed that she would leave the hotel in the early hours of the morning. Kerry knew Andre would be sleeping off the celebrations after the exhibition and he would probably sleep until about 11 am. After David had left with her suitcase, she rang reception and asked them to book her a taxi to City Airport, as she was returning to Paris. She booked the taxi for 7.30 am. The reason she asked the receptionist to book the cab to the airport was that if Andre called down to reception he would be told that his wife had taken a cab to return home. Kerry could not let Andre find out about David, or that she was staying on in London.

That night Kerry could not sleep at all for excitement. She could not believe that on her first visit back to London in ten years she had met David and was going to be staying in his apartment.

David took the taxi back to his apartment with Kerry's suitcase and her red roses, as he did not want Andre to see them and get suspicious. He was in shock. He had only attended the exhibition because one of his patients had given him a ticket as a thank you gift because she knew he was interested in art. David liked paintings, but he wasn't that keen on art or art exhibitions, so he had gone reluctantly. How different he felt now! He was ecstatic that he had met Kerry again. He could not wait for her to come to his apartment.

Immediately David returned to his apartment, he put Kerry's suitcase in the guest bedroom and started cleaning. He hoovered and polished and put new Egyptian sheets on the double bed. He then cleaned the en-suite and put new bath towels on the heated towel rail to keep warm. He put her roses in a vase in her bedroom. He managed to find some candles and put them around the room, so that it looked welcoming and warm. He really wanted to make Kerry feel safe and relaxed.

Then he started on his bedroom. He put the sheets from his king-size bed in the washing machine and put on clean ones. After he had finished his bedroom and en-suite he started cleaning the lounge and kitchen. He even made sure his fridge was clean, and threw out any out-of-date food. All this took him a few hours, but he was pleased to be keeping busy as it helped him to stop worrying about Kerry. He just wanted to make sure that his apartment was perfect for her. He showered and went to bed content in the knowledge that tomorrow would be arriving soon and bringing with it his Kerry.

The next morning Kerry woke at 6 am, showered and dressed. She gently opened the communal door to Andre's bedroom and saw that he had fallen asleep on top of the bed, still in his evening suit and snoring. Beside him was an empty bottle of champagne – and a blonde woman.

She locked the door again in case he woke up and came in to see her. She then started to write him a letter once again requesting a divorce and said she was returning to Paris, where she would be contacting a solicitor to draw up the necessary paperwork. She wrote that she hoped the exhibition would continue to go well for him. She put the letter in an envelope on her bedside table for him to find when he woke up. She unlocked the door that led to his room and left the hotel. Her taxi was waiting for her, and she asked the driver to take her to David's address instead of the airport. Kerry was so relieved to be in the cab and excited about seeing David again. She felt as if she was 20 years old again.

David had been awake since 6 am too. He was

panicking that Kerry might not still come. By 7 am he had showered, dressed and shaved. He managed some toast and coffee, then sat reading his newspaper while he waited for her arrival. So many thoughts were going around in his head. Where was this going to lead? Would they find the spark they once had or had it been put out forever? He decided that for now he was just going to enjoy Kerry's company as a friend, and if it went further then he would cross that bridge when or if he came to it.

Meanwhile during Kerry's cab journey the same thoughts were going around her head too. When she finally arrived at the apartment she loved it, much to David's delight. He made her coffee and toast and they sat out on his balcony in the warm sunshine overlooking the Thames. They seemed so relaxed together, and Kerry felt for the first time that she was home.

They enjoyed a few more days together before David had to return to work. He reminded Kerry how to get around London and gave her his Oyster card to use. Kerry loved London and realised that she had really missed living here. She greatly enjoyed her shopping days. In the evenings they went to the theatre and had some lovely meals out in the most beautiful restaurants.

Kerry then decided it was time to think about how she was going to get the divorce organized. David knew of a friend who had a solicitor in Paris, so he contacted him and asked him to draw up the papers for Kerry. A few days later they arrived and Kerry signed them. She then posted them back to the solicitor, who sent them by special delivery to Andre at his studio. Kerry could only imagine how cross Andre would be when he received them, although she was pleased that she was not in Paris when they were delivered.

Kerry wanted nothing from Andre except her freedom. Because there was no division of wealth or property, it was a very straightforward divorce.

After the exhibition in London, Andre had returned to Paris a very wealthy man, but when he received the official divorce papers, he was furious. He had searched everywhere for Kerry but had been unable to find her, so the arrival of the divorce papers was the first he had heard from her.

Eventually he calmed down, and began thinking that maybe it was the best thing to happen. After all, he had made himself a millionaire, thanks mainly to Kerry's paintings. He didn't really need her any more, and if they stayed married she was legally entitled to half the money from the exhibition. Although he did feel that he had treated her badly, she had remained loyal to him and his art.

So he reluctantly signed the divorce papers and posted them back to the solicitor. He then went to see his own solicitor and arranged his will, leaving the art studio and any unsold paintings to Kerry in the event of his death. Then he did what he always did; he went out and got drunk to celebrate his wealth and his freedom and slept with whoever he wanted.

After a few weeks Kerry got confirmation from her solicitor that Andre had indeed signed the documents. She was delighted. She soon decided, after discussing it with David, that she would like to stay in England. She also made inquiries to see if it would be possible for her enrol at college to get her teaching certificate in art so she could teach it in the local school. David was delighted.

When the divorce was finalised, David took Kerry on a boat ride up the River Thames to celebrate. They had a five-course meal with champagne on board and listened to a jazz band. While they ate, they watched the beautiful landmarks of London pass by, all lit up ready for the Christmas celebrations. It was magical and romantic. Kerry could not believe how happy, and how lucky, she was to have met David again after all these years. She then reflected that she had probably always loved him.

David was thinking the same thoughts. It was at this point that he got down on one knee and asked Kerry to marry him. He then produced the most beautiful and biggest emerald green engagement ring Kerry had ever seen. "I bought it because it reminded me of your beautiful green eyes," he said.

Kerry gasped in delight. She was so happy that she immediately said yes. "I would love to marry you, David" she said, and she leaned forward to kiss him.

# AFTER THE FUNERAL

⁓

As she gazed out of the window watching the rain and the wind blowing the leaves on the tree on that October day, Mary thought that the weather matched her mood completely, for here she was, a woman in her middle 60s, and today she had just buried the man who had been her husband, friend and lover for over 40 years. She was completely lost. Was it only last week that Andrew had been alive? He had seemed so well. No one could take in the sudden shock of his death. A massive heart attack and he was gone. No warning; one day healthy, the next day gone. And now the house was full of people in black clothing, all coming up to her saying how sorry they were for her loss and asking if there was anything they could do to help, or just saying, "Ask, and it will be done", as if somehow they felt this would help.

Mary wanted to scream and say "Can you bring back my husband and can you take away this awful pain that I have in my heart?" but instead, she nodded and smiled and politely said, "Thank you very much for coming". Soon they would all be gone and the house would be quiet again and night time would arrive. She would be able to stand here in front of this window, alone and feeling as desolate as the dark sky.

This window that she and Andrew had looked out together over the countryside so many times now seemed as despairing as she was. How was she ever going to cope without him? Would she always feel as lonely as this? He had given her two wonderful children, but they had their lives to live, and she did not want to be a burden to them.

They had enjoyed a good life together, travelling in their car to various places on holidays, and now Mary felt that all that had ended. What on earth was she going to do with the rest of her life?

She felt that the years had been kind to her, but she could not help admitting to herself that she was now rather plump and her hair was starting to turn grey. She always tried to look nice, but she was not the strong, independent type like some women. Andrew had been the strong one. He had been the one who had made all the decisions, and she had just followed wherever he had suggested they should go. She had been happy with this arrangement. Maybe she had been too happy to let him decide on everything, because now here she was unable even to decide what to do tomorrow.

Andrew had seen to the running of the home and their finances. Mary didn't have a clue about the bills. She was shocked to realize how utterly useless she was.

Her bed became her refuge, as she felt safe under the duvet, away from the world. Here she could dream that everything was the same, because that way she would not have to make any decisions for all the days that followed. Her routine was the same: bed, book, coffee, bathroom. She answered calls on her mobile phone from the children and said she was fine and not to worry, she was just having some rest. Little did they know that she hardly left her bed, except to use the bathroom.

In order to feel comfortable, she put all of the pillows around her. This made her feel secure. She was happy being surrounded by the warm duvet and reading a book, of which she had plenty, so she could escape her reality. She did this for several weeks after her husband's death.

Then, one day, the doorbell rang. Normally she didn't answer it, but she could see it was the postman and if she didn't open the door he would only keep knocking. So very slowly she pulled herself out of bed and went downstairs.

She was amazed at the amount of post on the floor. In fact she had to wade through it in order to open the front door to the postman. He had a parcel for her, which of course was for Andrew. She took the parcel and the many letters up to her bedroom and started to open them.

Most of them were sympathy cards. Did they really have this many friends? Most of them were from acquaintances of Andrew. He was very popular and outgoing, so perhaps she should not be surprised that so many people had sent cards. He was obviously going to be missed by many other people besides herself.

She went downstairs for another coffee, and realised that she was completely out of food and milk. She did not feel up to going to the shops, so she switched on her laptop and logged on to a supermarket website. She was very nervous about ordering on line, but Andrew had it all set up. She started adding things to her basket: milk, sugar, coffee etc. She was quite pleased, although she only ordered a few essential things in case she had done it wrong. Anyway she wasn't hungry, she just wanted some snacks to have with her coffee, but she was pleased that she had managed to do the shop on her own for the first time.

She chose a time for later on that afternoon for her food to be delivered. As soon as it had arrived she went back to bed with a packet of biscuits, a bar of chocolate, a hot coffee and a hot water bottle.

She had just returned to her book when her mobile phone rang. It was her daughter Jane inviting her to come for Christmas.

"When's Christmas?" Mary asked.

"Next week, Mum. Have you forgotten?"

Mary was appalled that she had completely forgotten about Christmas. That would explain the amount of post. Some of it must have been Christmas cards, but because the first few cards she opened were all sympathy cards, she presumed the rest were too, so she hadn't yet opened them.

Christmas was always Andrew's thing. He put up all the lights and the decorations and the tree. He loved Christmas. In a panic, Mary realised that she had no Christmas gifts for her daughter and son or their children. Andrew always bought the gifts.

Mary went on her laptop again and ordered some flowers to be delivered to Jane, a hamper for her son and games for the twin grandchildren. After that she went back to her book again, pleased that she did not have to go out to the shop and could stay in bed.

Then she remembered the package she had signed for earlier in the week, addressed to Andrew. When she opened it, she found it was a beautiful white fluffy dressing gown with matching mule slippers. It was Andrew's Christmas present to her. There were also some new white pyjamas, a big box of luxury bubble bath body lotion and some shampoo which smelt of coconut. She was overwhelmed that Andrew had thought to get her such a lovely gift. Inside was a small card with a short message which read "Dear Mary, Happy Christmas, love from Andrew". That was when she started to cry.

After she had finished crying, she realised that it had been weeks since she had had a bath or changed the bed linen, so she decided that today she would strip the bed and put new bedding on. She would then have a bath with the beautiful luxury products Andrew had given her and wear her new pyjamas. She did wonder if she should wait for Christmas day to wear them, but she felt it was right to use them now. That would at least fill up some of her day.

After her bath, Mary felt a little better. Maybe, just maybe, she would ring her daughter later on and say she would come for Christmas Day, just for a few hours. Then the post arrived and the postman asked her to sign for some documents, which she did. On her way back she stopped in the kitchen for her usual cup of coffee, then returned to her bed with the post in her hand. The writing on the envelope of one of the letters was unusual as it was addressed just to her, so she opened this letter first.

As she read it, her eyes opened wide in shock.

*Dear Mary, I hope my letter finds you well and that you do not mind me writing to you, but I have been very worried about Andrew. He is not answering my emails. He said he had a sister called Mary living at this address, so I thought I would write to you to ask if you could let me know if he is ok and maybe ask him to give me a call. My telephone number is 01486 733067. I am staying with my parents at this address until the 1st January and the reason I need to hear from Andrew asap is to confirm that our holiday is still on for the 6th January. I look forward to hearing from you soon. Kind regards, Sarah.*

Mary read the letter five times. She was confused. Who on earth was this Sarah? And why was she talking about a holiday on 6th January when Andrew had told her that he was going away on a business trip then? Could it be someone from his office? But Mary was sure Andrew's boss and colleagues would have told this woman about Andrew's death. They were all at the funeral, although Mary could not remember much about them. She knew she had been introduced to his colleagues. She could not remember a Sarah, but then she had been distraught, so maybe they had been introduced and Mary had not realised who she was. But why did she think Mary was his sister? It was all very confusing. Maybe the girl had got the wrong person. She would have to call her and explain.

Then her eye caught the package she had just signed for, addressed to Andrew. She opened it and read the contents.

*Dear sir,*

*Please find enclosed confirmation for British Airways first class flight with champagne to Italy on Monday the 6th January at 10am returning first class from Italy on Friday the 12th January. I have also enclosed your hotel itinerary for yourself and Mrs S. Williams.*

*We hope that you enjoy your stay in Italy and if you have any concerns, please do not hesitate to contact me on the number provided. Thank you for travelling with Romantic Holidays.*

Mary was shaking. There was now no doubt that her letter from Sarah was not a mistake. Andrew had a girlfriend, and he had been planning to take her on a romantic holiday. There never was a business trip.

Mary felt sick and completely devastated. The tears began to flow again. She was furious with herself for not having had a clue about what had been going on with her husband. How could she have been so stupid?

At this point, the phone rang. It was Jane. Mary did not want to tell her daughter what had happened. She felt she had to protect her, so she lied and told her that she had a terrible cold, which she thought would lead to flu, so she would not be coming for Christmas; maybe if she felt better in the New Year she would visit then.

Jane was concerned to hear that her mother was poorly, but Mary somehow managed to persuade her not to visit as she didn't want to pass her germs onto her or the children. She told her daughter that she had plenty of food and medication and that bed rest was the best cure. Eventually Jane agreed and said she would ring to check on her later on in the day. Mary was relieved that her daughter had believed her story, as it was partly true. She did feel extremely rough, but not for the reasons she had told Jane.

Mary was wondering what to do next. Should she contact this Sarah woman and tell her about Andrew? She didn't know what to do, so she went back to bed, even though it was early in the afternoon.

She awoke to the sound of her phone ringing. This time it was her son Edward wishing her a Happy Christmas. Mary could not believe it was Christmas Day, but then she remembered the time difference; after all, he was living abroad. She managed to convince her son that she had the flu. He was a very busy surgeon and he was on duty over Christmas, so she did not want to worry him, but she did promise him that when she felt better she would visit him, and he was happy with this. Then his emergency bleep went off, so the call to his mother ended. Mary was relieved that she did not have to have a long chat with him, as she feared she might not have been able to control her tears.

She wondered how long Andrew's affair had been going on. She decided it was time to check his email account, just in case for some reason there had been a mistake, and she was the one Andrew had been planning to take to Italy. After all it could have been a clerical error -an S instead of M? And she only had a letter from a stranger to say otherwise.

She felt very nervous when she opened up his computer. Where should she start? She went to his email account, only to realise that she needed a password. She went through the names of her children, her grandchildren, Andrew's middle name, the pet name of their previous animals, all to no avail. Then she thought of typing 'Sarah', and the computer logged her in.

Mary's fears came flooding back. It was now clear that Sarah was real.

She started to look through the emails. They were all talking about how much they had enjoyed each other's company and how he could not wait to take her away for their first holiday together. From what Mary could see, the affair had been going on for about six months. She felt a little better that it had not been longer, but then she started to worry. Perhaps over the last 40 years there had been other Sarahs. But for now, this new information was enough to confirm that her fears were true.

She decided to compose an email to Sarah. After many attempts, she decided to write as if she was

Andrew. After all, Sarah was obviously unaware of his death. She wrote:

*Dearest Sarah, I am so sorry but I have decided to end our friendship and cancel our holiday. I have been given an opportunity to travel around the world and it's going to be a wonderful experience. I have given notice from my work and I have decided to travel and eventually live abroad with my sister. We have decided that we will not be returning to England. Therefore I would be grateful if you would not contact me again. I have really enjoyed our time together. You are a lovely girl, but you deserve so much better than me. I am so sorry, but it now has to end. I am at the airport waiting to depart for my next adventure. I hope you will forget about me and enjoy your life with someone new and exciting. Love Andrew x.*

Well it was partly true, thought Mary. He is far away, and there is no contact, and he has 'departed'. After a long pause she pressed the send button, closed down the computer and returned to her bed exhausted.

Mary woke up the next day feeling better. She decided that she must pull herself together. After all, what was the point of staying in bed feeling sorry for herself and crying over her dead husband, a man who was a traitor and a liar? Today she would take charge of her own life for a change, instead of relying on her memory of Andrew to see her through the day.

At that moment Mary saw the holiday confirmation letter, and an idea started to form. Why shouldn't she go to Italy? As soon as the thought came into her head, she told herself not to be so stupid. How could she possibly go to Italy? She had never even been into town on her own, let alone travelled abroad. Yet although many negative thoughts came into her head, she kept returning to this first idea. Why shouldn't she go to Italy? She could not stop thinking about it for the rest of the day. First she would ring her daughter and tell her that Daddy had made a surprise reservation in Italy for them to go on holiday together as a Christmas gift and to get some sun during the winter.

She rang her and told her the good news, but Jane was not happy.

"You can't go Mum. How will you cope on your own?" she said.

"I must admit I was thinking the same," Mary replied. "But I'm sure this is what Daddy would have wanted me to do."

She went on to explain to her daughter that she

had phoned the travel agent and they had said it was all right for her to take the holiday alone rather than lose the money which had been paid in advance. Her daughter could not argue with that and reluctantly agreed that it would be a good idea, and that she would take her to the airport. That way she would at least know that her mother would get there safely without the worry of ordering a taxi.

By the end of the conversation her daughter had agreed to pick her up on the day of the flight to take her to the airport. As soon as she rang off, Mary started shaking. What on earth had she done? How would she cope with going to a foreign country on her own? But then, it was only a week, and what else would she do? Stay in bed and stare out of the same window every day!

So with her mind made up, she started to think about packing.

The day soon arrived. Mary's daughter was on her doorstep promptly at 7 am on the 6th January. They drove mainly in silence to the airport, each with her own thoughts and fears. If Mary had not been in the car with her daughter but in a taxi, she would have returned home, for what she was about to do really scared her.

Clutching her small suitcase, she kissed her daughter goodbye at the entrance to the departure terminal and waved her off smiling. Inside, she was shaking and wanting to cry, for she could not understand what had motivated her to make the decision to take this holiday. Had she finally gone mad?

She made her way to the desk, where a very nice young girl smiled and weighed her case. It was underweight, as Mary had packed only a few things. She was told to wait in the first class departure lounge. Mary had never travelled first class before, as they had very rarely gone abroad and when they had they had always flown in the economy seats.

Finally the time came for Mary to board the flight to Florence. She was shown to a comfortable seat all on her own and given a glass of champagne. She remembered to text her daughter to let her know she was safely on the plane. Then she accepted another glass of champagne. This really was the way to travel. She could get used to this kind of attention! For the first time Mary felt both contented and important, which she felt was probably due to the champagne on an empty stomach more than anything else.

After a further hour, lunch was served, with another glass of champagne. This time Mary made sure that she ate everything, as she was very concerned that she might get a bit tipsy before the landing if she did not eat. After living off snacks for the last few weeks, it was a treat to enjoy a roast dinner with all the trimmings.

Eventually she slept. She awoke, feeling much better, just as the seat belt sign came on for the approaching landing. She went through customs with her suitcase. Looking around the airport, she saw a man holding up a sign saying 'Romantic Holidays', so she walked over to the man and gave her name to him. He crossed her off his list, looking over her shoulder for her husband. Mary managed to convince him that her husband had suddenly been taken ill and had been unable to fly. She said that although she had wanted to stay with him he had insisted that she should enjoy this holiday.

The man seemed happy with this explanation and showed Mary to his waiting taxi. Mary was amazed at how quickly she had started lying to everyone. It was not like her, but she did not want to have sympathy or to be on this holiday with everyone feeling sorry for her. This was her adventure and she wanted to do it for herself.

She was amazed by the scenery of Florence. What a beautiful city it was. Eventually they arrived at the hotel, and that was beautiful too, and so very grand!

The porter took Mary's case and bags to her room while she checked in. She explained to the receptionist that her husband would not be joining her as he had been too poorly to fly. The receptionist asked her if she would still like to keep the same room, as it was the honeymoon suite. Mary was so shocked that she could barely say yes please. She had not expected this to happen.

She took the lift to the top floor, which was like a penthouse suite. Nothing in this world could have prepared her for the size of the room. It was like a whole apartment. There was a huge king-size bed, beautifully decorated in cream and gold, with French windows opening onto a private balcony. There was also a lovely cream and gold en suite with a jacuzzi. Never in all her dreams had Mary imagined a room like this existing, at least not outside a palace.

She then remembered that she had promised her daughter she would ring as soon as she had landed. She sat down and gave a quick cheery hello to Jane, then put the phone down and started to unpack.

That was when she saw on the table a beautiful bouquet of roses. She thought they were just part of the room decoration, but then she saw there was a gift card attached. It read: "To Sarah. I am so happy to be sharing this holiday with you. I hope you like the room, I chose it especially for you. All my love Andrew x."

She dropped the card to the floor and sobbed. She felt as if she had been stabbed in the heart. In fact she was convinced that the pain was a heart attack and that she was about to die, so she lay on the bed. She thought, well at least if she died it would be in a beautiful room. When she fell asleep, she fully expected not to wake up in the morning.

When she awoke the next morning she thought it had all been a nightmare. What else was this man going to surprise her with? She felt so betrayed.

There was a gentle knock on the door and in came a waiter with her breakfast. He explained that all the meals had been booked in advance, but because she was on her own he was giving her a single portion rather than a double and hoped that was all right with her. She nodded and said "Thank you."

Much to her surprise, she really enjoyed the breakfast. She raised her glass of fresh orange juice and said "Cheers Andrew, and thanks!" She even managed a smile.

She spent the rest of the day in her room on the balcony. It gave her a beautiful view of the red rooftops of Florence, and the sun was shining. She had a feeling that she was going to like Italy.

At breakfast the next day, the waiter said Mary was welcome to come down for the evening meal which had been provided and that they had arranged for a single chair and table to be put by for her. Dinner would be served at 7.30 pm.

Mary was in a panic. Dinner in a dining room on her own! She had never thought of that. All the holidays she had been on with Andrew had been self-catering or bed and breakfast, with a take away in the evening. They had eaten out only occasionally. She did not know what she should wear either, as she had brought very few clothes. What on earth was she to do? She was now shaking, and very upset. She should never have come on this holiday. What was she thinking? She could never cope on her own here. She must return home as soon as possible.

Then she glanced over and saw the hotel's brochure and welcome pack still unread on the table. She opened it and found that the hotel had shops, including women's fashions. Could she be brave enough to pop down to the lobby and see if there were any clothes to wear, even if it was just for that evening's dinner?

Eventually she decided to go and see. After all, what was the harm in just looking? She grabbed her handbag and went to explore the shops. She found a shop she liked and managed to pick out a dress that suited her. The assistant was very helpful and took her to the changing room. But to Mary's surprise, the dress was far too big. She had not even realised that she had lost weight.

The assistant found her a smaller size, which fitted beautifully. She also brought another dress in a different colour for her to try on. When she looked at herself in the mirror wearing it, Mary felt good about herself for the first time since Andrew had died. She decided to buy the two dresses and some white trousers, which she knew would go with the few tops she had already packed.

After purchasing her gifts with her credit card, she went back to her bedroom feeling very pleased with herself. By the time dinner time arrived she had had a bubble bath and put on her new dress. She was ready to go down to dinner, but she felt sick and shaky at the thought of dining alone; after all, nearly everyone at the hotel was with someone else.

Mary felt very sad and cross that her Andrew had put her in this situation, but then she realised that it had been her decision to come to Italy, so she might as well go down to the dining room. After all, it was only a meal. So with renewed courage she set off. A waiter escorted her to the table, which Mary was grateful to find it was in a corner by a large plant, so it was not so obvious that she was a woman dining alone. Fortunately the meal passed fairly quickly and without incident, and she was pleased to be finally going back to her room again.

When she arrived at her room she was surprised to see an envelope on the floor which had obviously been put under the door while she was at dinner. It was an invitation to go on a coach tour around the surrounding areas of Florence in three days' time. The trip had already been paid for by her husband, so her place was still reserved if she would like to be at the hotel reception lobby at 9 am. The tour would include lunch and they would return to the hotel at 4 pm.

Mary was horrified. There was no way she could possibly go on a day trip all by herself. She would be bound to get lost. Once again, she was plunged into the depths of despair, telling herself that she was just a weak, pathetic woman who couldn't even go out on her own for the day. She was so unhappy.

She eventually managed to ring down to reception to say that she was unwell and would not require breakfast in the morning. Then she put the Do Not Disturb sign outside her door and locked the door. She cried herself to sleep that night.

Mary woke up in the morning feeling unhappy that she was still alive. She really thought that during the night she would have died of a broken heart. Oh why was she here? Why had this happened to her? All these thoughts were going around inside her head. She felt that life was very unfair to her. Did she really deserve this? After all, she wasn't a bad person – was she?

Eventually she went out onto her balcony, sipping some water from a bottle from the mini bar fridge. She loved sitting out there on the balcony before everyone woke up. It was so peaceful and calming. The view was just lovely at this time of the morning. With a deep sigh, she began to read her book.

The day passed very uneventfully. Mary finished her book, then went back to sleep in the afternoon. She was awoken by her bedside phone. It was reception, asking if she would be dining tonight. Mary said that she would not be, and went back to sleep. Sleep was the only place Mary could rest her mind from all the conflict that was churning away. Sleep was the best cure.

Later on that day Mary once again noticed the invitation for the coach trip. She had resolved not to go, but what else was there for her to do? She had finished reading the books she had packed with her. All she could do was stay in this room for another day and look out of her window, which was exactly what she had been doing back at home. Why come to Italy if she was not going to see it? Soon she would be returning home. This was her last chance to see this country.

She decided that she would go down to the lobby to say she would be going on the coach trip and could she have an alarm call for 8 am. After she had done this, she was very worried that she had done the wrong thing, but it was done now so she started to get her clothes ready for her trip out. After all, it was only a day. The worst case scenario was that she could get lost, but then she would be with a coach party, so surely someone would realise she was missing.

With this in mind, Mary decided to get some sleep. At least while she was sleeping she would not be worrying about the trip.

The next morning her phone rang informing her that it was 8 am. For a moment, Mary could not remember why she was being told this, and then she realised that today was the dreaded coach trip. She really wanted to just turn over and go back to sleep, but then a knock on the door made her get up for her breakfast tray. Eventually she got up, showered and put on the clothes she had laid out ready to wear; the white trousers and pink T-shirt. She put on some sun cream and tied her hair up in a bun. Then she grabbed her handbag and left her room. She was in the lobby at 8.50.

Whilst she was waiting she saw some English magazines, so she bought a couple to take with her, thinking that at least she could bury her head in them if she didn't want to talk to anyone. As she approached the till, she also purchased a bottle of mineral water and some mints for her journey. She was now ready to board the coach. Fortunately some people had already boarded, so she chose her seat in the middle near the window. She put her handbag on the seat next to her in the hope that no one would sit there. The last thing Mary needed was some stranger talking to her.

When the bus started, Mary was pleased and relieved that she had the seat to herself. For the first time in a long time, she started to relax. The guide explained the day's itinerary and started to give information about the various places they would be passing on this trip. Mary started to feel happy. She had never been to Italy, and the scenery was breathtaking. They passed little villages. Some were very poor and some very wealthy, but the scenery was just beautiful. For the first time, Mary was really pleased that she had not missed out on her opportunity to see this lovely country.

Eventually they stopped for a photo opportunity and toilet break. Then they moved on to a little town called Sorrento, where you could see oranges and lemons growing from the trees on the roadways. The guide had said that they would be stopping here for two hours, and Mary was delighted. She did not go too far from the coach because she was worried about getting lost, but she did start to look in the souvenir shops for gifts. She managed to buy a few gifts for Jane and her grandchildren. She loved the kitchenware and the decorations of lemons on blue background on all the vases and bowls. It was such a cheerful place, with all the lemons and oranges growing wild, and the people in the shops were so friendly and welcoming. She thought she could easily live here in this lovely town.

At one o'clock, Mary met with the rest of the coach party for lunch at a small restaurant on the roadside with little patio umbrellas and check tablecloths. She managed to order a pizza with the help of the guide, Teresa, who interpreted for her, and for the first time she really enjoyed eating her meal and was pleased that the tour guide sat at her table. Teresa was a little younger than Mary and also single, and for the second time today Mary was pleased that she had come. She was also very impressed with Teresa. She was a very nice woman and so knowledgeable. She explained that she too used to live in England, but she had come out to Italy to do this job 10 years ago when she was 40 and has not looked back since.

Mary could not believe how courageous Teresa was to come to a strange country on her own. She was in awe of this woman who at 40 had decided that she needed a change. Teresa explained that she had taken Italian lessons at a night school with the idea of visiting Italy for a holiday, which she had, and loved it so much that she decided she wanted to emigrate there on her return from her holiday. She had seen an advert for this tour guide job, applied for it and got the job.

Mary was thrilled to be able to hear this woman's story, although at the same time it reminded her of her own failings and how she could not do anything on her own. Yet here was this woman living her dream and on her own. Mary wished she could be that courageous, but she knew in her heart she could never be that brave.

Soon it was time to leave and head back to the coach. Mary was starting to get a headache, so she decided to pop into the shop and buy a sun hat. She also got some paracetamol to take with her water and returned to the coach.

After more sightseeing, the coach returned back to the hotel. Mary thanked Teresa and went back to her room with her new purchases. She felt much better, but totally exhausted. When she looked in the mirror, she was amazed to see that she had caught the sun and that her skin was very red, probably that was why she had the headache. She decided to have a wash and change, then put on some after sun cream and rest on her bed until dinner time.

She eventually went down to dinner and enjoyed a delicious pasta meal before returning to her bedroom to think about packing her suitcase for her trip back to England. She wrapped the souvenirs in with her clothes so they would not break on the return journey, then rang the reception to ask for an alarm call for 6am.

For the rest of the evening Mary sat out on her balcony enjoying the cool breeze with a glass of wine from the mini-bar and watching the stars until she was ready for bed.

As the plane left the runway, Mary felt a tinge of sadness to be leaving this beautiful country. Admittedly she had seen very little of it. She was pleased that she had gone on the day trip but annoyed with herself that she had missed out on so much during her stay because she had stayed in her room all day. Even though it was a beautiful room, she did feel a pang of disappointment that she had not been brave enough to fully immerse herself during her holiday because she was still grieving for the loss of Andrew.

As she waited for her daughter to meet her, she realised that she had forgotten how cold it was back in England. She had only been gone a short while, but the temperature had dropped and there was a heavy frost on the ground and a slight mist. Mary shivered. Was it just the cold weather, or was it impending gloom at the thought of going back to the cottage where all her memories were?

Jane was pleased to see her mother and remarked on how brown she was and how well she looked, saying that it had been good for her to get away from the cold climate. She then proceeded to inform Mary of all the news within the family and said she needed to make an appointment to see the solicitor for Andrew's will to be implemented. Mary's thoughts of

Italy suddenly vanished, and she found herself slipping back into the dreadful darkness that had engulfed her before she had left. How was she going to cope with all the finances? And what if Andrew had left Sarah money in his will? How was she going to explain that to her children? If he hadn't made a will it would have been so much easier, as everything would automatically have come to Mary. That man had a lot to answer for! As soon as Mary was alone in the house again she began to cry. She did not know what to do.

A little later that day, Andrew's solicitor rang to arrange an appointment for Mary to come and see him regarding Andrew's will. They arranged an appointment for 2 pm the next day.

The following day, Mary ordered a taxi to take her to the solicitor. She felt sure that the solicitor must be able to hear her heart pounding as she waited for him to get Andrew's will.

It appeared that the mortgage had been paid off on the cottage, which had been left to Mary. There was also a savings account for their children and a trust fund set up for his grandchildren when they reached 18. Mary was pleased that Andrew had provided for her children and grandchildren, but she did not feel she would be able to stay in the cottage because it was in that home that Andrew had used his computer to cheat on Mary. She was grateful however that because his affair was relatively new, he had not thought to change his will to accommodate Sarah. A small blessing, she thought. However, she could not imagine living on her own with so many memories. Mary just did not know what to do, so she returned to her bedroom, where she fell into an exhausted sleep.

Soon it would be Easter; buds of daffodils and tulips were beginning to appear. It was the start of new life everywhere, yet for Mary, nothing much had changed. She had seen most of the winter from indoors, through the window. Now that the sun was beginning to appear she was pleased to think that she could soon be sitting in the small garden to pass some of the long daytime hours. She wondered if this was how it would be for the rest of her years, looking out of the window or sitting in the garden alone. She was feeling the hopelessness of it all. Maybe it was time to start clearing out Andrew's things and giving his clothes to charity. Then she would sort out his office. At least that would give her something to do during the spring.

While she was sorting out his clothes, she felt something in the pocket of his jacket and found it was a key with the number 26 on it. She decided to see if there was any paperwork in his desk drawer that would help her to find out where this key belonged. To her surprise she found a letter from the lottery organization, congratulating Andrew on a win of £200,000.

Mary was stunned. Who was this man she had been married to for 40 years? She thought they had had no secrets. She was appalled, and ashamed of herself for trusting him so completely.

The letter was dated last August, two months before his death. She felt sick as she put the letter back in the desk. She had to find out what had happened to this money.

Over the next few weeks Mary was like a woman possessed as she searched everywhere for the money. Eventually she remembered that Andrew was always pottering in his shed. Surely he would not hide the money there? Yet it was the only place she could think of where she had not already looked.

After a little searching she came across a small brown leather suitcase with the number 26 on it. She placed the key in the lock and sure enough, it opened. Inside, in a sealed plastic bag, were many bundles of fifty-pound notes, all tied together with elastic bands. She couldn't easily count it, but it certainly looked as if it could be £200,000. She was elated that she had finally found it.

She took the case back into the cottage and with trembling hands, she poured herself a large glass of wine. Her first thought was to redecorate the cottage completely. She could change it so much that there were no visual memories of Andrew. But then an idea came into her head. She didn't have to stay there. She could move and buy a new house instead. But where?

She saw on the sideboard a straw hat she had bought in Italy, and the memory of her holiday stirred once more in her heart. Could she possibly live there? After all there was nothing for her in England now. Yes, she would miss her daughter and her grandchildren, but they had only just started boarding school, so she would only see them in the holidays anyway, and they could always come over to stay with her in Italy during their holidays. She started to feel excited, something she had not experienced for a very long time.

The next day, Mary switched on the computer and started looking for properties in Italy. After searching for some time, she came across a beautiful villa in the village she visited on her day trip. She clapped for joy. She could not believe she had found this gem. Could she really do it? Could the woman who never left her bedroom possibly move to Italy?

Over the next few days, all these thoughts were swimming around in Mary's head. Finally, exhausted, she decided to talk to her daughter. Jane thought it was a great idea. She agreed that the children would love to visit Italy during the school holidays. They would learn some of the culture by visiting Italy rather than just reading books or doing research on line, and it was only a couple of hours away on the plane.

When Jane saw the pictures of the villa on the computer, she fell in love with it just as Mary had done.

"But are you sure you can afford it, Mum?" Jane asked.

"Yes darling, I have plenty of savings," said Mary.

At least this was partly true. For the first time she saw Jane looking at her with a real sense of pride. Was the old Mary of years gone by finally coming back? Mary thought she had lost her forever, but maybe, just maybe, she was finally coming through the dreadful experience she had been through. Could Italy be the place where she would finally find healing, and perhaps be herself again?

A few weeks later Mary and her daughter went to

view the villa, and they both loved it. The village people were welcoming, and Mary felt she had come home, although she had told Jane that it would only be a winter home. Mary knew in her heart that this was where she belonged, where she could be accepted for just being herself. She decided to buy the property and use it as a holiday home for the time being, until she could decide if she wanted to move there more permanently.

Back home in England she researched Italy and bought a course of Italian lessons on CD so she would at least be able to communicate, however poorly, with the local community.

Before long it was the 6th October, the first anniversary of Andrew's death. She decided it was time to go and visit his grave. As she stood beside it and said her last farewell to him, she felt she was closing the chapter to her old life. She reflected over the last year and realised that the woman who had stood at this graveside a year ago, completely distraught, had now gone. Mary was able to hold her head high and get ready to move on to the next new adventure with a feeling of happiness that she had not felt for a long time.

At the end of November, Mary visited the villa

with Jane. They went shopping, buying beautiful pottery with lemons on it for her new kitchen, which she decided to decorate in blue and yellow. The villa already came beautifully decorated, and it was also furnished, but Mary just needed to add extra touches to make it feel more like home. She bought some beautifully embroidered furnishings for the bedrooms and lounge. She was so pleased to be sharing the experience with her daughter, as it had brought them much closer together during the last few months.

Mary started to prepare for her first Christmas in Italy. Her family joined her for the Christmas holiday, and it was wonderful being with them again. Although it was now December, it was a warm evening, so they decided to have a barbecue around the pool. She watched her grandchildren splashing with their father in the pool as Jane filmed the fun they were having. She glanced over towards her son, who was cooking on the barbecue. He was looking so relaxed. She knew she had made the right decision, not just for her, but for all of them. She hoped they would have many more of these lovely days here together.

Her children remarked to each other later on that evening on how different their mother was compared to a year ago. In their hearts her son and daughter both knew, although they did not voice it at the time, that Mary was here to stay, and they were happy for her.

Soon the New Year was upon them, and Mary was invited to spend it with her new neighbours. She was overwhelmed at how readily their families had accepted her and on the stroke of midnight they were hugging her and wishing her a very happy New Year. A toast was raised to Mary, the newcomer. They wished her good health and happiness in her new home and country.

Mary felt blessed, but also saddened that Andrew was not able to spend his last days in this beautiful village with the most loving and generous people she had ever met. She was also pleased that her children still had good memories of the father they had loved and had been spared knowledge of his indiscretions. She reflected on how different it would have been if Andrew had not died. Would she be divorced now? Although she didn't understand it at the time, this really was the best solution for her. She raised a glass of champagne to Andrew, the man who had bought her home, to Italy.

A year later Mary returned to England to sell the cottage. Her daughter and son helped her to sort out all the things they wanted to keep and hired a skip for all the unwanted items. After the sale of the property, which took quite a while to sort out, Mary gave half the money each to her son and daughter; she wanted nothing from the sale of the property for herself apart from a few personal items which held fond memories for her. Both her children were working hard and the extra cash meant that they would have a better lifestyle. She wanted to see them enjoy it while she was still around to see it. After all, she had her beautiful villa fully paid for from the lottery money, and she still had a good amount of money in her bank, so she was very comfortably off.

Mary was amazed at how a year could change someone's life. She could now speak Italian relatively well. She had joined the local church and was very involved in the women's circle and enjoyed being able to help those less fortunate than herself. For the first time, Mary felt fulfilled, and that her life had more purpose than it had ever had before.

As Mary boarded the plane for her return journey to Italy, she felt an excitement and a happiness she had never experienced before. She could not wait to be home again. She reflected that however dark your experiences are in life, there is a silver lining to most situations. To experience the light, sometimes you have to go through the darkness. From the woman who felt she could not cope with life after losing her husband had emerged the woman she really was, strong and resourceful. Although she still went through sad times, most of her days now were very happy indeed.

# A BABY ON THE DOORSTEP

It was a wet and windy evening when the doorbell rang. Across the road, Emily was sitting at the bus shelter waiting for the bus. She held her umbrella so that she could not be seen, but could clearly see the house opposite. As she got onto the bus, she saw the door of the house open and a lady take in a parcel. Inside this parcel was Emily's baby.

Emily was pleased that her plan to leave her baby on the doorstep at this house had worked, so far. She got off the bus at the next stop and started to walk toward a block of flats. She entered the flats and went up to a bedroom on the first floor. The flat was empty because it was waiting for the council to come and redecorate it.

Emily then changed her clothes. She took off the black outer clothes she was wearing, stuffed them into a bin liner and pulled on a bright red coat. Then she put on a long blonde wig and took her clothes with her. She departed from the flat through the rear entrance, where the car she had hired was parked under the shelter of a very large and overgrown hedge.

Emily put her bag in the car and left the car park with the lights off to avoid detection from any possible cameras, just in case the police had been called. Once she approached the main road, she put her headlights on and proceeded to the airport. She parked the car in the hire car park and left the keys in the office. Then she took the black bag with her clothes in and put them in a recycling bin just before the airport. She took off her wig and put it into a carrier bag, which she stuffed into another bin. After this, she then went into the ladies' toilets at the airport and turned her red coat inside out so that it became a white coat. She then put her own long dark hair up in a ponytail and put on some lipstick. Picking up her suitcase, she then went to the check in for her flight to America.

So far, so good. All she had to do now was be herself and get into the queue for her flight.

Emily was relieved when she had finally boarded the plane. She was soon up in the air and leaving England behind her, with a very heavy heart. Feeling exhausted, she shed a tear. Fortunately she had booked a night flight, so she could rest.

The following morning, she arrived at the hotel in Florida where she had booked a three-week holiday. Her holiday was fully inclusive, with spa and treatments, so she could relax after the trauma of giving birth. She had an English paper delivered to her suite every day and was pleased that there was no mention of a child being left abandoned in England. It appeared that so far her plan had worked out very well. At last she could relax and try to enjoy her holiday.

After three weeks in the sun, Emily was pleased that her figure had almost returned to normal and she was looking very healthy and feeling relaxed, with an amazing tan. She had her hair trimmed and checked out of the hotel to return to England. It was a Saturday afternoon when she arrived back at her suite, after taking compassionate leave for six months to look after her brother, who had cancer. Well, that was the story she gave to her boss and colleagues and how she chose to keep her pregnancy a secret. She did not even have a brother.

Emily had her own office in Canary Wharf and worked as PA to a company director. She loved her job and worked hard, but she didn't have many friends or attend any social engagements outside of work. She was never off sick, hardly ever took any annual leave and had never had any serious relationships because of her personal circumstances. Her job was all she had.

That was until she had gone to Germany nine months before for a conference. Emily had booked into a small hotel near where the conference was being held. It had been a very long, boring day and she was exhausted. She returned to her hotel, which she had chosen in preference to the one her colleagues stayed in, because she preferred to be alone. She had booked in under a false name.

She had never been to this part of Germany before, and she needed some time when she could, for once, just be herself.

After having a few drinks in the bar she had found herself flattered by the attention of the barman. He was German, with fair hair and blue eyes, and he was called Kurt. He was very kind to Emily, making sure she had plenty of drinks and food. He was very entertaining and Emily instantly liked him.

She could not really remember going up to her room. She had had far too much to drink, which was very unlike her. It was also not like her to let her guard down. She felt for the first time in years safe and free to be herself.

In the morning when she woke up, she felt happy as she remembered the amazing romantic dream she had experienced. Then she turned over. She was horrified to see Kurt asleep next to her. Obviously it was not a dream; she had actually slept with him. Thank goodness nothing had happened.

Very slowly and quietly, Emily got up, showered and left the bedroom. Thankfully she only had a small flight bag with her, which she had already packed the night before. She crept out of the bedroom at 6 am, grateful that Kurt was still fast asleep. She paid her bar bill with cash and got a taxi to the airport. She arrived back in England and proceeded to make her report of the conference, so that she would be ready for work on the Monday.

A few weeks later, after working every night until 8 pm, Emily began to feel extremely tired and nauseous. She put this down to the workload she had experienced over the last few weeks. She eventually made an appointment with her GP to see why she was feeling so ill. He examined her, then asked if there was any possibility that she could be pregnant.

She laughed. "Doctor, you have to have sex to have a baby and I have not had sex for years, So the answer is no," she said.

Upon hearing this, the doctor told her to come back for further tests in a week's time if she did not feel any better. In the meantime he prescribed vitamins and rest, saying as it was probably a virus she had caught.

On her way home Emily thought about what the doctor had said and was suddenly caught by the memory of Germany. Surely she hadn't actually had sex with Kurt? Surely she wasn't pregnant? Or was she? How could she be so irresponsible?

She decided that on her way home she would go into the chemist and buy a pregnancy test, just to be sure. On her return home she took the test, and it was positive. She was eight weeks pregnant.

Emily was in shock. She stayed in bed all day being sick, mainly from worry. Pregnancy was not an option for her. She would have to have an abortion, but she had heard so many horror stories of people dying or catching dangerous infections after having abortions. Besides she was a Catholic, so she could not imagine doing such a thing.

It was during Mass the following Sunday that Emily decided that she would have the baby and have it adopted. However she was determined to choose the family herself.

Every evening during the spring, Emily would visit places where she felt her child would enjoy growing up, preferably with a loving family. During a walk in the park one day she sat down on a bench with her book to read. Just then a woman appeared with her daughter, who was about three or four years old. The little girl asked her mother if she could have another sister or brother, to which her mother replied "No darling, Mummy cannot have any more children because after you were born Mummy was very ill and had to have an operation and she can't have any more children."

The child replied, "So can we have a puppy instead then?"

The mother smiled and said, "We'll talk about it tonight when Daddy comes home."

This seemed to settle the child's inquisitive questions. The woman and the little girl left the park bench, and Emily smiled to herself. She really liked the mother and child and decided to follow them at a safe distance. They were so happy together, the little girl skipping beside her mother. They were totally unaware that she was following them. She watched as they went into a nice semi-detached house on a main road with a bus stop opposite.

After seeing them that day, Emily sat most evenings at the bus stop to watch the family come and go. They seemed such a lovely family, always happy going to the park together, so Emily decided that they would be just the right people to adopt her own child.

That was when she decided that once her own child was born, she would leave it there for them to find on their doorstep.

Now she had found her family, she decided to do some research on them to make sure they were suitable. She found that the father was a local dentist and the mother a part-time teaching assistant at the local school, where her child attended nursery. Emily decided it was time to take action and plan her next few months. After a lot of research, she booked herself into a private hospital so she could plan when her child would be born, by caesarean section. She also started to create a new name, address and lifestyle for herself.

She decided to go with the story that her husband was a naval officer, to explain why he was not with her for the appointment and scan; she would say he was at sea for long periods, sometimes many months. She needed it to be believable, so that she could not be found out after the birth.

She went on the computer and found a photograph of a naval officer aboard the HMS *Independent*. He had fair hair, blue eyes and a kind face, although he was a little older than Emily. She decided he would become her pretend husband, so she printed his picture and put it in a frame on her bedside table. Emily decided to call him Kurt Richmond, as Richmond was the surname of her child's new family to be.

She then found a cottage to rent for six months which was very isolated, but cosy. It was a one-bedroomed cottage, and it was near the private hospital where she would be giving birth.

Emily decided that now was the moment to inform her boss of her desire to spend time with her brother. He was not too happy with this, but he could not protest too much as Emily had hardly ever taken annual leave or sick leave over the five years she had worked for him, and she was owed six months' holiday anyway. He decided to find a temp to cover Emily's work before she left, so that the work could continue in her absence.

On her way home, Emily informed the doorman, George, at her hotel suite that she was going to look after her sick brother in Wales for six months. Then she said that she was going on holiday for a rest after looking after him, and would George please keep an eye on her suite for her. She did not leave a forwarding address. She would see him in a few months, depending on how her brother responded to the chemotherapy. She then paid her rent for a year to the hotel, just in case there were any delays in her return. She paid in cash. Emily always paid in cash for everything.

Emily then went to her safe and took out a telephone number, one she had not rung for more than five years. It was the number of a friend at Scotland Yard. He was very surprised to hear from her, and even more surprised to learn of her request.

After telling everyone of her brother's sudden illness at work, she cleared her desk and said she would be in touch when he had recovered. Not many people were interested in Emily, as she was very quiet and never showed any interest in their lives, so they didn't show any interest in hers now, which suited her. She always had to keep a professional low profile, but she longed to be carefree, and now she was excited to be getting out of the office for a few months, which surprised her considering that she really did enjoy her job.

She eventually arrived at her cottage in Wales. She attended her anti-natal appointments for scans and blood tests etc. Everything was going very smoothly with the pregnancy, and she was enjoying a restful time in the cottage.

On her next visit to the hospital an appointment was arranged for Emily's caesarean section. She had everything in place in the cottage for the birth. She bought limited things such as basic nappies, baby milk, bottles, vest, one-piece baby suits, blankets, a hat and a small straw Moses basket.

She only stayed in hospital for 48 hours and said that she would be returning home to her cottage with her sister, who was going to stay with her for a few days. After that she and the baby were going to live with her parents on a farm in Cornwall to recover while her husband was away at sea.

Once she was back in the cottage her 'sister', who was in fact an undercover policewoman, handed over to her the documents she had requested. They were the adoption papers for her son, whom she named William Kurt Richmond. He weighed 6lbs and he was beautiful. He had fair hair and blue eyes and Emily loved him.

Eventually, with a heavy heart, Emily signed all the relevant papers so that it was legal, including a birth certificate, which the policewoman gave her. She then wrote a covering letter to the new parents of her son William.

*Dear Mr & Mrs Richmond,*

*I would be very grateful if you would sign these adoption papers and bring my son up as your own because I am unable to look after him myself as I am in a Witness Protection Programme, so it would be very dangerous for me to look after him. I would appreciate it if you would not mention this to the police or any member of your family or friends. For your own safety I would advise that you say you applied to a private adoption agency for adoption and that they arranged for you to adopt William.*

*Please keep all the relevant paperwork I have given you including all my medical details. (Unfortunately I do not have any of his father's details except that he is German and he was a very kind man.) I can assure you that these documents are legal. I have also enclosed some money which I hope will go towards the cost of caring for William. I have also organised a trust fund for him and your daughter when they both reach 18. I have observed that you are a lovely family and I know that you will give*

*William the best life it is possible for him to have. I in return promise you that I will never get in touch with him or you again as it could endanger his life and your life, so in advance I thank you and ask you to give him a wonderful life with your daughter. Thank you from the bottom of my heart, for I truly do love him.*

*Kind regards,*
*William's birth mother.*

After writing the letter Emily then arranged her flight, car hire and hotel for her trip to America.

Life returned to normal after her trip to America, and for two years Emily worked hard, trying to blot out the memory of her son. After that, she decided that she would return to the park to see if she could catch a glimpse of him. On a lovely Saturday afternoon, she sat on the bench with her book. She stayed for a few hours waiting and hoping she would see him again.

At last, after what seemed like an eternity, Emily heard a little girl's voice shouting "William, stop!" Emily turned to see a little boy running after a squirrel with his older sister, mother and father following him laughing. It could only be William, her son. They seemed very happy.

Eventually William was scooped up in the arms of his father, laughing and playing. It so touched Emily's heart to see her child so happy that she began to cry tears of happiness.

She wished she could take a video, or a picture, of him on her mobile phone, but she knew it would be too dangerous.

At that moment William came running up with some bluebells in his hands. He stopped with a big grin and offered them to Emily, and she thanked him. Then she glanced up and she saw that William's mother was approaching. She too was holding some bluebells, and she smiled as she came over.

"I am so sorry, but my little boy loves bluebells and he is always giving them to everyone" she said. "I hope you are not offended."

Emily smiled and assured her that she was delighted to have the flowers. On leaving the park, she placed the bluebells in her book. She was so happy that she finally had something of William that she could keep forever.

Just then Emily's mobile phone rang, and she listened intently to the caller. Then she rang off and made her way hastily out of the park. That evening she placed the bluebells into a little photo frame, wrapped it inside a hand towel and placed it under her clothes in her suitcase.

The next day Emily handed in her notice at work. She informed her boss that she had been given a wonderful opportunity to work for a financial adviser in New York, but she had to leave immediately to start work there. Needless to say her boss was not happy, but Emily reminded him of the girl who had done her job until a few years ago. She still had her details and had already contacted her. The girl was willing to do Emily's job permanently, and she could start immediately if her boss was agreeable. Fortunately he agreed, and after working her last few days in her office Emily went home to pack. She emptied everything from the flat. Then, putting on Marigold gloves, she wiped clean the entire flat, making sure no fingerprints were left anywhere. She said goodbye to George on her way out to the taxi.

As she went through customs with her boarding pass for the flight to New York, Emily was stopped and escorted to a back room. There she was told that as it was no longer safe for her to stay in England, instead of going to New York she was to be relocated to Australia. She was given a new passport, a new identity under the name Anna and documents which included the paperwork for an apartment in Sydney.

On her arrival in Sydney, Emily was pleased to find she had a very nice apartment overlooking the sea. As she started to unpack, she was delighted that her bluebells were still safe in their photo frame. She then started to look on the internet for posters of bluebells, and bought one with lots of bluebells surrounding a tree. She was delighted with her purchase and placed it on her living room wall. Then she placed the bluebells her little son had given her in the photo frame on her bedside table, so she would always have a reminder of him. It was something she could keep with her throughout her life, wherever she was. She kissed the picture frame goodnight every night, with a prayer for his health and safety.

Emily – or Anna as everyone now knew her - started a job as a waitress in a small tea room. She felt content and happy for the first time, because she knew that whatever happened to her in the future, she had a beautiful son enjoying his life to the full, a gift which she had given him, and that he was safe and happy. She never returned to England, but she always took the day off work on William's birthday and went to the local park for a picnic.

A couple of years went by and she was given the

opportunity to buy the tea room, as the owners were retiring. She was delighted. She decided, however, that she would add an extra area for an ice cream parlour. She worked hard getting the little tea room ready. She had it beautifully decorated, and she loved seeing all the children coming in with happy smiling faces to choose their favourite ice cream. She decided to change the name of the tea shop to "BLUEBELLS" in memory of her son. She bought a little teddy bear and had its name embroidered on its blue T-shirt – 'William'. Then she put it on display on the counter. Now, whether she was at work or at home, Emily would have a constant reminder of her son.

# THE JOYS OF RETIREMENT

It was a cold blustery autumn day, and the sailing ships were bobbing up and down on the sea. Eileen had never felt so cold in her life, even though she was all wrapped up against the cold. Why had she come to this godforsaken place anyway? What on earth had possessed her to come here? True, she had wanted a holiday, but in the middle of January?

She felt she had lost her mind completely. Having desperately needed to get away, she had found a cottage by the sea and thought it would be good for her to have walks along the sea front. How wrong she had been! She had only been here a day and had never felt so lonely in all her life. It was far too quiet for her. There was not a soul about, probably because they were all tucked up in their nice warm cottages.

Yes, the cottage boasted a real fire, but she hadn't realised that she would have to see to it every day if she didn't want to die of hypothermia. She was very cross at herself for not doing more research into this country escape idea. In her mind she would have been sitting in front of a roaring fire, having lovely walks along the beach and drinking nice cups of coffee in the nearby village. Instead she was in the middle of nowhere.

She had got the train into the main town of Exeter, then ordered a taxi to take her to the cottage, which took an hour. So, when she had eventually arrived, it had been evening, it has been dark and she had been very tired. The cottage was cold and dark too, but Eileen was exhausted after travelling for hours, so she just got into her pyjamas and laid on top of the bed and fell asleep. In the morning, she woke up to the sound of chickens clucking. It was pouring with rain and there was no food anywhere to be seen.

She thought that at least the owners could have left her some milk or bread for her arrival. She was not impressed. She decided to light a fire, but that was just useless. She put the coal on and found some old newspapers, but there were no matches or candles. Eileen was so cross. This was not like the brochure at all. The advert had said: *"lovely cosy cottage in the middle of glorious countryside, with a large open fire, free range chickens in the garden which will lay eggs for breakfast. Local pub which serves good food daily. Including lovely views of the sea and walks"*. Well, that had sounded very nice to Eileen. In reality, it was a tiny one-bedroom cottage with no heating apart from the fire, which she couldn't light because there were no matches. So she decided to go out for a walk to the local shop to get some food in, only to find that it was closed due to the bad weather! The pub where she hoped to have lunch was also closed, as the owners were away for the weekend.

So here she was walking along the beach in the rain and wind. What on earth could she do now? She kept walking and eventually came across a bus stop, but she found to her horror that the bus only came once an hour. So there she was, getting wetter and colder by the minute, and now she had to wait nearly an hour for the bus.

When it eventually arrived, she asked the driver how far it was to the next village, as she needed some food supplies. "Oh my lover," he said, "it's only three miles away." So she boarded the bus. She was sure that the surrounding countryside would be nice if she could just see out of the windows in this rain!

Eventually the driver told her that she was to get off, as this was the stop she needed. Eileen followed his directions. She spotted the bakery shop first, which pleased her. She bought two loaves of bread and a few doughnuts for her tea. Then she went to the newsagent's shop and managed to get some matches and candles and some magazines to read. After this, she went to the mini-market shop for more supplies. She now had four large carrier bags to hold as she waited on the other side of the road for the bus to appear.

It was another half hour before Eileen boarded the bus. By then she was even wetter and even colder. Again the driver told her where her stop was and she managed to walk for another 15 minutes. Just when the cottage came into view, one of the bags split! Great, thought Eileen, just what I need, soaked through and all the food on the ground.

She gathered up her shopping and eventually arrived at the cottage looking like a tramp. "So much for country living" she muttered to herself. She eventually managed to light the fire and change into some dry clothes. She then put some soup on the hob and enjoyed her fresh bread with cheese. At last she was warm and had food.

She decided to stay in her cottage the next day. Then she remembered the chickens, so she went out and collected six eggs. That evening she made an omelette, which she ate with a steaming mug of coffee, followed with doughnuts by the fire, which was now roaring. She felt much better. It's amazing how much better you feel once you are warm and fed, Eileen reflected.

Later she managed to watch TV. It was only a small set, no Sky or Wi-Fi here, but she was happy with the few channels she had because it helped pass the time. Then it was time for bed, but Eileen decided not to go to bed as it was so cold everywhere in the cottage, apart from the lounge, so she built up the fire again and lit the candles she had bought. Then she brought the duvet and pillows down and went to sleep in front of the fire on the couch as she watched a late night film.

The next day it was still raining and windy outside, so she stayed in the cottage reading her books and magazine and watching daytime television. The following day was no better, as it was still raining, so she decided that she would start writing a novel. She had her laptop, although she could not get an internet connection. She started to write, but she was not really inspired. She had thought that by coming to the country she would feel alive again, and this would bring her the inspiration to start a novel. She had always promised herself she would write one day, and this seemed like the best opportunity to see if there was a writer inside her. Unfortunately for Eileen, this was not the 'Escape to the Country' she had envisaged.

She was still hungry, so she went out for a walk to see if the pub was open. She was delighted to see that it was, and it was serving lunch. She ordered a roast dinner and enjoyed a delicious apple pie and custard. The locals were friendly, but they were not really interested in a woman sitting in the corner eating her dinner alone.

Eileen felt so isolated. Everyone here knew each other, and she felt like an outsider. It wasn't long before she went back to her cottage. This was not the country retreat she had planned.

Eventually Eileen decided that she would return home. She had always dreamed of moving to the country, but she now felt that this idea had not been realistic. In the small town where she lived, everything was on hand for her. She could easily get into

London, where she had free travel on the Tube and buses. Although she didn't have many friends, she did have good neighbours, and they were always pleased to see her.

For many years, Eileen had been a matron on a busy hospital ward. She had never married or had children. Her work was her life, and she loved it. She did not have many friends, because she never mixed socially with other people outside or in the hospital. Other members of staff were always going out and having fun, but Eileen was married to her job. She never went away on holiday. The annual leave she did take was involved with arranging staff duty rotas, attending study days at work or doing interviews for new staff. At home, Eileen spent her time organizing any jobs such as repairs or decorating her flat.

She had always felt when she retired that she would like to move to the country and write a novel. She thought the best place to move to was by the sea, which was why she had booked this mini holiday. Of course, she thought to herself, if she had done it in the summer, then maybe it would have been a better experience. She appreciated that this was England, and it often rained, but she had never experienced a cold wind like this before.

She wished she had made an effort to make more

friends, instead of living for her work every day. Now she had reached retirement age, she had nothing to do and no one to share the rest of her life with.

She returned to her flat with a heavy heart. There was very little post on the mat when she arrived and, with a tear in her eye, she realised that no one had noticed that she had been away for four days.

Although Eileen was very pleased to be back in her familiar surroundings, she realised that she was going to end up a very lonely woman if she did not do something about her life. Her job had totally dictated her life, and now there was no job she felt she had no life.

She was grateful to feel the central heating warming her home, and although she felt lonely, she was very pleased that at least she had a lovely warm flat. And at least she had good health and wasn't in an old people's home… yet.

This spurred Eileen to go onto her computer. She wanted to see what local groups there were which she could join. She found some sites for over 60s, but most of them were gardening or cookery clubs, which Eileen could not imagine herself joining. But then she saw a group called The Yellow Hats. This group was for everyone, male or female, as long as they were over 60 and were, or had been, professional people who wanted to be part of a group. They went on outings to the theatre and museums etc.

This, thought Eileen, was just what she needed. She registered on line and asked for a brochure and newsletter to be sent which gave information about all the events taking place locally. When the newsletter arrived, Eileen was pleased to see that they also went out on day trips and that they always wore yellow hats. This made her laugh. Could she really be part of a fun group at her age? She had always been so serious with her job, but she did giggle at the thought of the directors' and managers' reaction if they saw her sporting a yellow hat.

Eileen decided to go along to the next meeting, just to see if it was her cup of tea. She was pleased that the Yellow Hats met in a nearby café. She arrived there and immediately spotted them, because of course they were all wearing their yellow hats. They immediately welcomed Eileen to the table, where they ordered a coffee for her. This evening was just for new members and Eileen was pleased that there were four other people joining that night, three ladies and a man. The group consisted of ten people, and they were all very friendly and polite.

Eileen really enjoyed their company and decided to join the group, which met every Wednesday afternoon. At the meetings they had coffee and cake and then discussed arrangements for their next outing.

Eventually the day came for Eileen to go to the community hall for her first meeting. On arrival she was amazed to see about 40 people gathered. It was a very jolly afternoon and everyone was getting out their diaries to start filling in the events. The chairperson welcomed Eileen and the other new members to the group, after which everyone clapped and smiled. Eileen felt she was going to be happy here.

They all wrote down in their diaries the various dates for forthcoming trips. The next was going to be a theatre performance in the West End with afternoon tea. The chairwoman then spoke to the new members and asked them about their hats. She said they had a lady who designed them, Mrs Chappell, and she would be willing to make them in any style they wanted. Eileen made an appointment to have her hat made the following day.

When she arrived for her appointment, Eileen was amazed at all the material Mrs Chappell had. She had been a milliner, and although she had now retired, she still liked to make hats, so she was delighted to be given the task of making the hats for the group. She explained that yellow had been chosen as it was a bright, cheerful colour. Other colours were allowed as well, but they had to be brightly and tastefully done.

"We don't want to look like a fuddy duddy group out for the day," said Mrs Chappell. "We want to look as if we are having fun."

Eileen decided on the style she wanted and chose to have a big white daisy on the side. It was beautiful, and she really enjoyed wearing it. The members only wore their hats during the journey to and from the event, unless it was in a museum, so they could all recognise each other and stay together. Once they arrived in a restaurant or theatre they put their hats away.

Eileen loved the first visit to the theatre and the afternoon tea in Fortnum & Mason was just divine. There were 20 in the group. They always split the groups, as 40 was too big for them to all go out together, so you just chose the event you wanted to go to. The lovely thing about this group was that you could change your group at any time. If you did not fancy a particular event, you could go out with the other group.

After she had been in her group for six months, Eileen decided that she would go on a mini-cruise with the whole group of 40 people. She was excited to be going on her first holiday with so many lovely friends. Tomorrow she was going out shopping to buy herself some new outfits, including some evening dresses for her cruise. Eileen was really enjoying her retirement now. She had not yet had time to write her book. Maybe one day she would make a start, but for now she was going to enjoy every day.

Eileen knew that her days of being alone and staying in remote country cottages were finally behind her. She decided that she was going to keep a scrapbook of all her days out. She bought a new camera and took lots of photos of the group outings. On cold or wet days, she would work on her scrapbook and smile as she looked back on all the lovely memories she was making. As she left to go out for lunch with the ladies from the group, she decided that her views had changed over the past months. Retirement, thought Eileen, is just wonderful.

# REVENGE

—◦⁓◦—

Agatha was furious. She had put her faith in the justice system, and it had failed her miserably. She could not believe that the judge could not see that she was telling the truth.

Well, she would just have to seek her own justice. After all, she had played it straight. She had got a very good solicitor and barrister who believed in her, yet still her family, if you can call them family, had won the case against her, leaving her penniless and having to pay their court costs too.

Agatha had been adopted into an Italian family, as their second child. After the birth of their son,

Signor and Signora Pica had found that they couldn't have any more children, so they decided to adopt. But Agatha had never really fitted into the family. They looked upon her as "not of their blood", and treated her like an outcast.

She lived a very lonely life. She went to school in the local village, but made few friends, as they always laughed at her name, not being Italian like theirs. Her brother Carlo, on the other hand, was very popular and the house was always full of his friends. He behaved very badly, but his parents could not see what he was really like. Although Agatha was a much nicer and kinder person than her brother, they constantly found fault with her.

Eventually, Agatha went to senior school and then to university in England. Her parents did pay her tuition fees, but Agatha felt they really just wanted to get rid of her, rather than being interested in furthering her education. She loved the university in Bath and she loved the city and settled in well. The people were very kind to her and she made some good friends.

It was during her last year at university that she had a phone call that was going to change her world forever. Her brother had been killed in a car crash, and she was to return to Italy immediately. She was met by great hostility from the family on her arrival, even to the point where her mother cried "Why couldn't it have been Agatha and not my lovely adorable Carlo?"

This really broke Agatha's heart. She asked why she had been made to return if they did not want her there, and was told that her uncle had also died in the car with her brother and that after the funeral they would be holding a family gathering to read his will. It appeared that Agatha had been left a small sum of money. She was shocked that she had been left some money by her uncle, but he had been the only one who had been kind to her and she was very moved that he had thought of her in his will.

After the double funeral, the will was read. It appeared that her uncle had left his little villa to Carlo, but his larger villa, which was on the outskirts of Rome, was to go to Agatha.

Agatha was very moved at the kindness of her uncle, but her mother and father argued that it would not be appropriate for Agatha to have the villa and that it should go to her father's brother's son instead. Agatha was mortified. Why could she not have the villa, she asked?

Signora Pica turned to her and laughed. "My dear girl, you are not Italian and there is no way that you, an English girl by birth, could ever inherit any property in Rome!" she said. She went on to say that such a thing was unheard of, especially as she was a girl, and they felt her uncle must have been suffering from dementia when he wrote his will. They insisted that the solicitor should pass the villa and the necessary paperwork on to the only other boy in the family. They agreed only that Agatha could keep the money that had been left to her.

Agatha protested. She told the solicitor that he was not to fulfil this request, and that she would get a solicitor of her own to contest the will. She stayed on for a few weeks and attended a ceremony in the town where a statue of Carlo was placed by the family as a shrine to his memory. Agatha felt sick. If they only knew the real Carlo!

Agatha returned to finish her last year studying chemistry at Bath University, and was awarded a First Class Honours degree. She used the money from her uncle to find a good solicitor and barrister to bring her family to court. As she was English, she decided to proceed in England.

It took Agatha two years to bring her case before a judge, who read all the statements from her father and mother and other members of the family. A letter was also provided from their local GP saying that her uncle was suffering from the early stages of dementia. However, the GP was a cousin of her father!

After two days going through all the legal documents, the judge declared that Agatha had no rights to the estate and closed the case. Agatha was distraught. It was then that she decided on revenge. She would change her name by deed poll, as she wanted no connection with her family ever again. She changed her name on all her documents and had a new passport issued in her new name. She chose the name Andrea Johnson. To her family in Italy she was still Agatha Pica; they would not know of her new identity.

Agatha went back to Italy and rented a small one-bedroom apartment in Rome, where she started working in a chemical laboratory and became one of their top technicians. While she was working on a particular poisonous chemical, she started to think of ways in which she could get back at her family. Obviously she did not want to kill them, but she did want them to suffer.

Signor Pica was very proud that he owned a lot of land. It was his pride and joy to look out of their home and say to everyone "I own all of this land as far as the eye can see". He was always bragging about it as if he was some kind of lord, and everyone agreed that it was wonderful. His land and his son were the only things Signor Pica was proud of.

This gave Agatha an idea about how she was going to get her revenge. She thought about how important her parents' reputation was to them. Agatha knew Carlo had taken many photos and videos of himself and his friends messing around, drinking and taking drugs. She had found them when she had gone into his room after the funeral, and taken them in order to prevent Signor and Signora Pica from finding them. She had packed them in her suitcase and forgotten about them – until now. She decided to send them to a newspaper anonymously, saying they were from a friend of Carlo's.

Even she was surprised a few days later to see the photos on the centre spread of the newspaper with the headline "LANDOWNER'S SON WAS HOOKED ON DRUGS AND ALCOHOL". Could he have been drunk or on drugs when he crashed the car in which he and his uncle were killed?

When she went to visit her parents the next day to see their reaction to the news, she found a crowd of reporters outside the property. Signor and Signora Pica were telling them that this was just a smear campaign to bring dishonour to their son's memory. It was a very convincing act.

Agatha realised that this idea was not going to work. She was going to have to hurt them where it would hurt most – through their money. Without money they would have no prestige in the community, and prestige was everything to them.

Whilst she was visiting her parents she told them she was working in a chemist's shop in Naples, which did not impress her parents, as they saw working in a shop as beneath them. She then mentioned to her father that he should consider selling the land to a developer to have lots of houses built there. Imagine the money he would make on it. He could build hundreds of houses on the land, and he would be a multi-millionaire when it was all finished.

Signor Pica dismissed this idea at first, but then he grew more interested. He said he would consider looking into finding a developer.

"I must admit, it's a good idea" he said. "But Andrea, don't think that when your mother and I die you will inherit anything."

Agatha was very hurt by this remark, and she asked him why he hated her so much. He said he didn't hate her, but she had to be punished for taking them to court. For the first time he told her of her birth, and what had happened when he had first brought her home from the convent. His wife and everyone in the family and the community said he should have got an Italian child and not an English one, and that she should have been given an Italian name after her mother's family. Her father went onto explain that he had chosen Agatha as he had heard there was a famous author in England called Agatha Christie, and he thought that seeing the parents were English it was a good name to give his baby. Unfortunately he had not bargained on the reaction of his wife and family in giving Agatha this name. They said they would never accept her.

Agatha felt a little better, knowing that it was not something she had done wrong. She had just she had the wrong nationality and name.

He said her parents had been English, but she had been born in Rome, where her real mother had been living. Apparently she had been the fourth girl to be born and the mother did not want her husband to know she was pregnant again as the child was not his, so she said she was going to work in Italy as they needed the extra money and her husband would stay in England with the other children. She had been a cleaner for the convent and lived there until Agatha was born, leaving the nuns to find a suitable home for her. Her father had heard that this child was available for adoption, so giving a very generous donation to the convent, he had taken her home with him.

This was the first time Agatha had heard this story. Now she knew that she would never be accepted. She continued to plan her revenge.

After leaving her family and making sure that she had all her belongings from her old bedroom, which were very few, she went back to Rome as Andrea, but to her parents, she was Agatha returning to Naples.

Happy to be back in Rome again, Agatha enjoyed reading and every evening she would go to the local library and get books. It was during this time that she came across a very old book on plants, and she became intrigued. She read that there were certain very rare Japanese plants that could poison land for many years. Agatha did not want to destroy Signor Pica's land, but she did want it to have the appearance of having been damaged naturally. She went back to the laboratory and started working on various chemicals to see if she could simulate the plant from Japan without it being harmful to the land or being detected.

A year after visiting her parents, she had made her chemical plant. She took a small quantity and went to her parents' land, making sure they were at Mass.

She took a long stick, went halfway into the field and placed a small amount of chemical all along the middle of the field. Then she covered the holes with the remaining soil.

After a couple of hours Agatha had completed her task. There was no evidence that anyone had been there. Satisfied, she returned to the rusty old Jeep she had parked nearby and returned it to the local garage. She had borrowed it from Antonio, the owner, without asking. He always had an early lunch and then an afternoon nap, and he always parked it around the corner from the garage and left the keys in the ignition. Antonio was always driving around the roads adjoining the land, so if anyone saw the Jeep they would naturally think it was him.

Agatha returned to Rome and waited for news. A few weeks later she had a phone call from her father saying that the grass on his land was dying. He was devastated and was thinking of sending a sample to have the soil analysed. Agatha suggested that he should send it to a laboratory in Rome to analyse the sample. Of course she gave him the address of the laboratory where she worked, saying that the boss she worked for in Naples knew that they could give him a report on any damage. All she had to do now was wait for the sample to arrive at her laboratory.

When the sample arrived she typed her report, saying that the land was useless and that no cattle or vegetable could be grown there for at least 50 years. She suggested that the owners move out, as it could be dangerous for their health. She also put a warning on the letter that the property and land could not be sold or rented and that it should remain empty for as long as the soil was contaminated. She used an official government stamp on the letter, addressed the envelope and sent it off to her father.

In reality the land was not at all contaminated. The chemical had just turned the land brown, but Agatha knew her father would believe the official report.

A few days later Agatha phoned her father to see how he was. He told her that the report was OK and the land was not contaminated, but they were going to be moving into his brothers' home as her mother was very ill with cancer and he had a heart problem.

A few months later Agatha heard that her mother had passed away. She did not attend the funeral. One day Agatha went to her parents' house to find everything covered in dust sheets. She went to her father's study and found some paperwork, including a letter from the judge saying he had ruled in her father's favour.

Agatha was horrified. She knew her parents were devious, but to bribe a judge in England to make the case go their way was beyond her.

She then came across a copy of her father's will. It was a new will which said that on the death of her father, as her mother had already passed away, the property and all the land was to go to Agatha, to deal with as she wished. Typical, thought Agatha. He had only left her the land and house because he thought it was worthless! He had left all the money to his brother.

Agatha was very pleased that she would be inheriting the land and the house, because she knew they would be worth millions, especially as there were no records anywhere of any contamination on the land because she had destroyed them, and it looked like her father had done the same.

She returned to Rome to work on another chemical. She needed her father to be confused, so that he would not return to the property, and in the event of her not inheriting the land she could claim he had dementia. Well, it had worked for her uncle, hadn't it?

Eventually she made a fine powder which made a person drowsy so that they were not sure what they were doing. Now she had to find a way to administer it without being found out. Her father loved Turkish delight, so Agatha got a box of it and rubbed the sugar into a bowl. She then put her powder in with the sugar and sprinkled it back on to the Turkish delight. It did not affect the taste, but it would make anyone who ate the Turkish delight feel drowsy - she tried it on herself and it worked. Then she posted the box to her father, saying she had seen it on a visit to Rome and thought he would enjoy it.

A few months later she heard that her father had deteriorated and wanted to return to his home to die. Agatha agreed to this and told her father's brother that she would take time off work to look after him, so this was arranged.

A few weeks later Agatha's father was back home in his bedroom, and Agatha was the perfect daughter. She looked after him well, making sure that he was well and truly drowsy. She also made sure that the local doctor visited regularly. However, just before the next visit from the doctor, she told her father what she had done to the land. He was very angry and threw a glass at her, but she ducked out of the way. Then he clutched his heart. At that moment she realised he was having a heart attack, and she ran downstairs just as the doorbell rang. It was the doctor. She opened the front door and told the GP that she had just heard a noise and thought perhaps her father had fallen out of bed

She asked the doctor to go up quickly because she was worried, although she already knew that her father had just had another heart attack. The doctor ran upstairs to her father and left Agatha in the hallway. Eventually he came down full of sympathy, saying he was very sorry but her father had died as a result of a massive heart attack and that as he was present he would deal with all the necessary details.

After the funeral the solicitor told Agatha that she had inherited the land and the house and gave her the deeds. The solicitor then gave a cheque to Signor Pica's brother. The brother was delighted; he had no wish to have all the land and house as he had his own land, and Agatha's father had been too proud to tell anyone about the contamination. She suggested that her uncle should take his family and go on holiday, maybe a cruise from Naples.

Six weeks later, while Agatha's uncle and family were away on their cruise, Agatha sold the house and the land to a property developer. There was no record on file about the contamination, as she had destroyed all the documents. The developer was planning to build affordable housing on the land for families who could not afford to buy their own property. She signed the papers and received a cheque for five million euros.

She was delighted. Not only was she very rich, she now had her revenge on her parents and on the local community. They would be furious about having a housing estate on their doorstep, as it would greatly affect the price and status of their own property.

Agatha left Italy for the last time and returned to Bath in England. She had enough money to buy a beautiful, chic apartment. She told the estate agent she was buying the property on behalf of a client, who was abroad at the time. She signed all the papers and transferred the money for the apartment to her new name. Then she ordered beautiful furniture to be delivered.

She was very happy with her new home and could not wait to settle in, but before she could do this she still had the matter of the judge to deal with. She decided to leave her beautiful apartment. She securely locked it, then turned on the video surveillance cameras and left.

She rented another room near the station in Bath to continue planning her revenge. She decided that it was time to do some research. She would see how best she could start destroying his career so that no one else's life would be damaged by him again.

She found out where his chambers were and managed to find a flat on the first floor overlooking the entrances. She then bought a second-hand bicycle from a student. The bicycle had a box on the back to take her things, including a safety helmet. Then she bought a single train ticket to London.

When she arrived in London, she mounted her new bicycle and followed the directions the landlady had given her to the flat. She paid two months' rent, explaining that she was there on a work visa and would be returning after that time. Every day she kept a log of the judge's schedule and noted the details. She then went to a back street IT shop and explained to the man in charge that she needed something that would enable her to read a password on a computer. She explained that she had just bought a new laptop and had put the password in, but because she had used it too many times the computer had gone into lockdown and she couldn't access it. She also said that the deadline for a job she wanted was yesterday and the company had stated that it had to be done on the computer on that date. Was there any way they could get the computer to put yesterday's date and time on a document?

The shopkeeper felt sorry for this sad-looking girl and said he would help her. He gave her a small gadget, explaining that all she had to do was plug it into the side of her laptop and it would automatically read the password and alter any date/time she wanted. It would cost her £100. The money was not a problem to Agatha. She paid it in cash and thanked him emphatically.

Now all she had to do was somehow get this device into the judge's computer. Then she would be able to read his password and get access to it.

She noted that the chambers used a cleaning company to clean the offices. She rang the number on the van parked outside and asked if they had any vacancies. Fortunately the man said they desperately needed someone for this Thursday from 9 pm – 11 pm, and also on Friday evening from 9-12, but it would only be for two nights while his other cleaner was ill. Because he was desperate to get cover, he said she could bring all her credentials and give them to him on Saturday afternoon when she collected her wages. Agatha agreed, because she knew she would be gone by then. She was delighted. She could not believe how well it was all going.

When she arrived at the offices for her cleaning job she wore big glasses, a ginger short wig and a head scarf. She always kept gloves on, so that none of her fingerprints would be found, and she kept her head down in case she was picked up by any security cameras.

She eventually got into the judge's office and managed to plug in her device into his computer. She immediately got his password. She then set about cleaning his office. On his desk was an open diary, where he had written that he would be away in Scotland until Tuesday.

The next day Agatha managed to start in the judge's office. She plugged in the device again, opened his computer and put in the password. She managed to find more than 50 pornographic sites which showed photographs of children. Once they were recorded in the computer's memory, she used the device that allowed her to change the time so that instead of saying 21.30 it would read 12.30, the time when the judge would have been at his desk. That was according to the schedule she had observed through her binoculars over the last few weeks. He always went to lunch at one o'clock.

When she was done she printed some of the photos of children and hid them in a book on his bookshelf. Then she quickly polished everything and made sure it was really clean. Her only worry was that his fingerprints would not be on the photographs, but she hoped that the police would assume he had wiped them.

On the Saturday morning Agatha left her flat and bought a single ticket to Reading from the ticket machine on the platform with cash. When the train got to Reading she left her bike at the railings and took the wig off and put it in her handbag. She then bought a single ticket to Bath. She eventually arrived home at her rented apartment in the early evening.

On the Sunday afternoon she took a train to Bristol Airport. She timed it for when the airport would be at its busiest, with people travelling for the bank holiday. She went straight to a call box, where she dialled 999 and said that Mr James Edward Hall of Hall's Chambers was known to be having sex with under-age children. She then hung up. She put the ginger wig in a bin at Bristol station and got the train back to Bath. Once home, she dumped all her clothes in the dustbin and cleaned out the rented flat, just leaving her new clothes out for the morning.

On Monday morning she went to a hotel spa she had booked and had all the works; a manicure, a pedicure, a facial and a body massage. She also had a full makeover and had her hair cut short and dyed brown. She hardly recognised herself in the mirror.

She would even go as far as to say she looked pretty, which was a big contrast to the girl she had been all these years. She had deliberately let herself go so that she would not stand out, and had only worn long skirts and baggy jumpers. Her long blond hair was tied in a bun, and she wore big glasses, all to hide who she really was. Those she worked with at the lab hardly looked at her twice. Now however, she was a sophisticated young lady.

On her way home she did some clothes shopping in Bath, bought a small Louis Vuitton suitcase, put all her new clothes inside and treated herself to a meal in town before heading back home to her beautiful apartment with her many luxury clothes and make up. On Wednesday she left her apartment again to fly to the Philippines, where she had previously sent money to build a new orphanage.

Whilst she was in the first-class departure lounge, the TV came on with a newsflash saying that Judge Hall had been arrested. Agatha smiled and boarded the plane for her flight. At last she could now relax. Even if he was not charged, he had been humiliated and his record tarnished.

On returning to the UK three months later, Agatha read in the newspaper that Judge Hall had been found guilty. He had been stripped of his title and would never work as a judge again. He had also had to pay a fine and was put on the sex offenders' register. Because the judge had pleaded guilty to going on porn sites and because he had never actually had sexual relationships with children, he was only given a prison sentence of three months. Agatha was amazed that he had pleaded guilty. She continued to read the article. It seemed the police had raided his home and found some real evidence. This was a big shock to Agatha.

Agatha greatly enjoyed her time in the Philippines. She was pleased that her money was being used to help children who were left abandoned through no fault of their own, and that it would eventually change many children's lives for years to come. She decided that on her next visit she would stay longer and work there, for there she felt she was valued, not just because of her money but as a person. This was a very unusual feeling for Agatha.

For now though, she was going to enjoy her new apartment and have a glass of champagne and a bowl of strawberries to celebrate the victory of her revenge.

# A GIRL CALLED BOY

———∽———

All Megan did was raise her eyebrows, and that was enough for her father to reach across the dining room table and grab her hair. He wound his fat fingers around it and dragged her up the stairs to her bedroom. Then he threw her onto her bed and left the room, locking her in her room alone, and went back to eat his dinner.

Megan was furious. Why on earth didn't her mother stand up for her? All she ever said was "Try not to upset your father, dear".

"Upset my father!" Megan had screamed, the last time it had happened. "I am the child, not him. Why don't you do something?" At which her mother gently stroked her hair and then left the room. Megan thought her mother was useless and vowed that one day she would make her father pay.

Megan could not remember the exact date when her father had started hurting her. It was always her hair, which was very long, and she was not allowed to have it cut. She usually had it in a plait or a ponytail, but recently she had noticed that it was falling out in places. This was due to her father. He never marked her or sexually abused her, it was always her hair. Megan was sure he did this so there would be no evidence of any bruises.

It had first happened one day when she was seven years old. Megan said she didn't want to sit at the table and eat her dinner with her parents, but instead asked if she could watch her favourite television programme. When she came downstairs the next morning the television had been smashed and thrown into the garden, and they never had another television again. Usually this sort of thing happened about once a month, but lately it had become more regular. Her father was always in a bad mood. Her mother never worked, but stayed home all day cleaning and cooking. She led a very solitary life, although she did occasionally talk to the neighbours.

At 10 years old, Megan was never allowed to bring any friends home or go to their homes, so she had very few friends to play with. Her mother took her to school and collected her every day in an old car, which was falling apart, but at least it was reliable. Megan thought this was because her father didn't want her speaking to anyone outside the family, if you could call it a family. There was only her and her mother and father. Her mother's parents were dead and her mother was an only child. The only other family left were her grandparents, and they lived a long way away in the north of England. They rarely saw them and all Megan could remember of them on the few times they visited was that they were very old and grumpy and hardly had any time for her. They were only interested in their son, telling Megan and her mother how proud they were of him and how lucky they were to have him provide such a lovely home for them.

Megan became very lonely. The only comfort she had was being allowed to read books and do her homework in her bedroom. She loved books, and she became very good at reading at an early age. Reading was a way she could escape into a world where she was never lonely or hurt. She loved fairy stories about princesses and she longed for her prince to rescue her as they did in her stories. Her favourite book was *Alice in Wonderland,* and she used to dream that one day she would be able to escape down a rabbit hole.

When she was not reading, she was wondering how she could hurt her father. She was full of hatred for him, although recently she had noticed that he was getting very fat and the idea of her being able to hurt him was becoming more unrealistic, so instead she started to think of a way of how she could escape from this house.

One day at school her teacher called her aside and said she had noticed that she had head lice and that her hair was getting very thin, and maybe it would be a good idea to have it cut. Megan said she didn't think that her father would allow her to have it cut as he liked it long. The teacher said she would give her a letter to take home to her parents explaining about the head lice.

When Megan's mother arrived at the school, Megan gave the letter to her. Immediately she took Megan to the chemist to buy some lotion. She asked her mother if it would be possible for her to get her hair cut too, as the teacher said she should. Megan's mother agreed that it had got very thin and long, so much so that Megan could now sit on it. So when they got home her mother rang the hairdresser's and made an appointment for Megan to have her hair cut after school the next day.

That evening, Megan's mother put the lotion on her hair. Megan had never experienced such pain in her entire life. The lotion really stung her scalp. The reason it was so painful was that when her father pulled her by her hair he always scraped her scalp with his finger nails. She was unable to sleep because of the pain, and her mother was very upset and gave her painkillers and put a cool flannel on her head. She kept saying how sorry she was for not standing up to her father, because she was very afraid of him too. She said she would try to be braver in the future and even leave him and live somewhere else. For the first time in a long while that evening, Megan's mother stayed until Megan fell asleep.

The next day when Megan woke up, she was excited about her mother's promise to leave her father, and about getting her hair cut. She hoped the hairdresser would cut it short so that her father would not be able to pull it any more.

As they approached the hairdresser's, Megan's mother wanted to pop into the local supermarket, so she let Megan go into the shop on her own, instructing her that she was just to get it trimmed to a manageable length. With this information Megan went into the shop and asked the hairdresser to cut her hair as short as possible. The hairdresser was shocked to see how sore Megan's head was and told her that maybe she had had an allergic reaction to the head lice lotion. She agreed that it would be a good idea to have it cut short. When it was finished, she saw her reflection in the mirror and was very excited. Her hair was now parted on the side and very short, about two inches all over.

She paid the money to the hairdresser and went to meet her mother in the supermarket. Her mother was horrified when she saw her. "What on earth has happened to your hair?" she asked.

Megan said that the hairdresser had mentioned that her hair was very badly damaged and that she still had some head lice, so she had no choice but to cut it all off. She also suggested that it would be best if it was kept short and she should come into the shop every three months to keep it tidy. Her mother seemed happier after this explanation. After all, her mother never challenged anyone; she was very accepting.

That evening, when Megan's father came home, he stared at Megan in disgust. Her mother explained what had happened, but he continued to stare.

"You look like a boy with that short back and

sides" he said. "From now on you will be called "Boy". During dinner he said to Megan's mother, "Tell Boy to get me a mug of tea now". He continued to call her Boy every day. At least he had stopped pulling her hair. Instead, he just insulted her every time he saw her.

Although his comments were very cruel, Megan was just pleased that he was not pulling her hair any more and that her scalp was getting better and less red and sore.

It was now time for Megan to start senior school. Her mother dropped her off at the gates and Megan went in alone. She hated this new school. All the children were laughing at her hair, calling her a boy and even asking if she was a lesbian. Not that Megan fully understood what a lesbian was, but she knew if must be something that was not nice in order for them to think it was a funny thing to say to her. Megan became very withdrawn, and although she did her studies and kept up with her work, she always sat at the back of the classroom and never put her hand up as she wanted to try to remain invisible. She did well in her work, but she was very lonely.

At the weekend, Megan's father said that now she was a boy, she should earn some money, and he said she could do a paper round to earn her keep (even though she was only 11). He got her an old rusty boy's bike with a tatty basket on the front. He then told her that she had to be at the local newsagents at 5am the next day.

Megan was delighted that she had a bike, because it gave her freedom and she was happy to get up at 4.30 am every day before school and at weekends. She loved being out in the fresh air instead of always in her bedroom. Every week she gave her father most of the money she had received from her paper round, but each week she kept £1 back and put it in a jar under her bed. This way she thought that when she and her mother finally left home she would have some money, although during the winter months she did sometimes spend the £1 on a chocolate bar or hot drink from the machine. This treat was wonderful for Megan.

She loved her paper round and enjoyed going into all the driveways of the houses. The houses were all so different. Some were very big and grand and had long driveways to cycle up and others were very small like her own. Some had lovely big cars on the driveways too.

It was during her paper round that it became apparent to Megan that her own house and family were quite poor. Nearly all the houses were beautifully painted and looked so nice and inviting. She started to dream about what it would be like living in such a beautiful house.

When she arrived home from her paper round, she put her father's newspaper on the table for him to read, together with her wages. Fortunately he never noticed that it was always a pound short. Then she went back to her room, putting the pound coin into her jar under her bed. She continued reading on her bed until it was time for her to dress for school. She never spoke to her father, as she did not want him to know just how much she enjoyed her paper round, otherwise he might stop her going.

Megan knew that her father did not intend for her to be happy. He regarded the paper round as a punishment, although to Megan it was freedom, and she could not wait for 4.30 am. It also meant that she was able to go to bed earlier in the evening, which meant she had to spend her less time with her father. This gave her an excuse to go to her room, so that she was up in time for her paper round. However, as soon as she was in bed, she read her beautiful fairy stories and dreamed of her prince until she fell asleep.

All the other children walked to school, and they were always on their mobile phones or iPads or talking about a recent television show. This only made

Megan feel more isolated, as she had neither of these things. However, there was to be an after-school programme to learn the basics in computing. Megan decided that she would sign up for the Friday afternoon club, as she really wanted to be able to learn how to use the computer. Also, Fridays were the days when her father always came home very late because after work he always went out drinking in the pub with his mates. She got permission from her mother, who said she would come at 5 pm on a Friday instead of 3.30 to collect her.

When Megan started her classes, she was very nervous, as she knew nothing about computers, but after she had explained to her teacher that she did not have a computer at home, he very kindly gave her extra attention in the class so that she did not fall behind. It was a rare treat for Megan to have someone be kind to her, and she really enjoyed her extra lessons on a Friday.

After a year of school Megan became very good at computer studies and managed to get an A grade for her hard work. She had never had an A before. She was excited to tell her mother when she collected her, but instead her mother was angry that Megan had kept her waiting for 10 minutes because she said she and her father were going out to the pub together that evening, and she did not want to be late.

It was very unusual for Megan's mother to go out with her father, as they led separate lives, but her mother said that tonight the group from her father's work were meeting in another town and her father wanted her mother to come, so that she could drive him home, because he wanted to drink. Typical, thought Megan. He is just using her as a taxi service.

Megan's mother said she didn't want to upset her father yet as she was planning to tell him soon that she wanted a divorce. Megan was delighted that maybe, just maybe, they would both soon be free. She was also pleased because she would be able to listen to the radio while her father was out. The radio was in the sitting room and it was always on the channel her father wanted to listen too. Megan and her mother were never allowed to listen to any other channels. So when her father was out, she and her mother would listen to the radio, remembering to put it back on her father's station afterwards. Tonight, however, Megan had the house to herself to listen to any station she chose.

At 2 am Megan was awoken by a loud banging on the door. She was very afraid and did not open the door until she heard the man say that it was the police. Very slowly she opened the door to see a policeman and a policewoman standing there. They said that they had some very bad news for her and could they please come inside.

They asked her to sit down and then told her that both her parents had been killed in a car crash. Megan could not believe this news and asked how it had happened. It transpired that her father had been driving and he was very drunk. The police said they thought her parents had been arguing at the time of the accident and that her father had not seen a turning and had driven into a wall.

Megan said that the reason her mother had gone was because she was going to drive. The policeman said that according to an eye witness in the pub car park, her father had insisted on driving and had been seen dragging her mother into the passenger side of the car before driving off at speed.

The policeman said they needed a family member to identify the bodies as she was too young to do it, and asked if she could give them the telephone number of a close relative. They also said someone would be needed to look after Megan. Megan explained about her elderly grandparents and went to the phone book and gave them their telephone number. Eventually she fell asleep exhausted on the couch. The policewoman put a blanket over her and said she would stay with until her grandparents arrived the next day.

When she woke up the next day, the policewoman was making a cup of tea, and she asked if Megan would like one too. At first Megan thought it had been a bad dream, but now she realised it was true. Her parents were dead! She was not at all upset that her father was dead, but she did feel very sad that her mother had died, just when she had managed to find the strength to leave him.

The policewoman informed Megan that her grandparents would be arriving soon and that they had already been to the mortuary and identified her parents' bodies. They would be coming for Megan that afternoon. Megan asked why they were coming, and the policewoman explained that they would be taking Megan to live with them on their farm.

This was a great shock to Megan, as she could not understand why she could not stay in the house on her own. After all she was nearly 13, and most of her life had been spent on her own in her bedroom anyway. The thought of living with her grandparents filled her with fear and she started to cry as she had never cried before. It wasn't just the terrible shock of losing her parents. It was the thought of leaving everything she knew and living with two grumpy old people. She was just devastated. Could her life really get any worse? Megan packed her belongings, which were very few. Her most precious possessions were her story books, the jar of £1 coins she had saved and some photographs of herself as a baby with her parents when they were younger. She finished off by packing all her clothes into a very old suitcase. Then she left the home she had known all her life to go and live with her unwilling grandparents.

It was a cold and lonely journey. After travelling many miles, they eventually arrived at her grandparents' home. It was a big farm with no central heating, and as soon as she arrived her grandfather made it clear that she was there to work. When she enquired about school, they said she would no longer be going to school. She was to earn her keep by working on the farm, and tomorrow she was to be up at 4 am to help milk the cows.

Megan unpacked her clothes in her bedroom, pleased that at least she had all her books with her to read. The bed had a big eiderdown on, which thick and warm. In fact she preferred this bedroom to her own, which was very small. At least this was a large room, and it had shelves so that she was able to have all her books out on view, rather than in a corner on the floor as she did at home. It was a very nice room, and she had a pleasing view of the farm from her window.

Getting up at 4 am was not a problem for Megan, as she was used to getting up for her paper round, but she found it much harder to milk the cows than delivering papers. The work was exhausting, although there was always the cooked breakfast from her grandmother which she had ready for her on the kitchen table to eat at 7 am, which Megan was really grateful for. Cooked breakfast was a luxury to her, and she ate well, so perhaps her life was not too bad after all.

However they still called her Boy; her father had told them it was a pet name he had chosen and she was to be called that in future, and of course they always did what her father wanted.

A year later, Megan's grandfather collapsed on the farm. Megan ran in and called her grandmother, but by the time she came her grandfather had already died of a massive heart attack. Megan knew now that her grandmother would want her to do more chores in order to keep the farm going. However, her grandmother did start to warm towards Megan and one cold winter's evening when there was deep snow outside, her grandmother asked her if she could knit. Megan said no, so her grandmother started to teach her. All through the winter she knitted squares and then sewed them together to make a blanket. On Christmas morning she wrapped it up and gave it to her grandmother, who was delighted.

It was then that her grandmother opened up a bottle of sherry, and as she drank the sherry she started to talk about her son. Needless to say, she had no Christmas gift for Megan, but she did tell her a secret which turned out to be the best Christmas present she could ever wish to have. She told her that she was not her father's daughter. Apparently her mother had had an affair with a young boy who lived in a nearby farm and had become pregnant. Megan's father knew it was not his baby as he was sterile from having the mumps as a child, but he said he would bring the child up as his own, provided she told no one, apart from his parents, and that she would never tell Megan's real father about the baby, or contact him again. Once her mother agreed, they moved to the south of England for work.

Now Megan began to understand why her father had hated her so much. She wanted to know all about her real father, but her grandmother would not discuss it. Megan decided to wait until another time to ask.

The following summer Megan's grandmother passed away. Megan, who was now 14, had been running the farm almost single-handed, along with a few farmhands who helped with the livestock and getting the cows to market. After the funeral, Megan decided to try to find out more about her father. She went through all her grandmother's papers, but could find nothing. She did not know what to do with the farm.

Eventually she found a letter addressed to her which her grandmother had written a few months before. It said that the farm did not belong to them but to a landlord, and they were his tenants. This was a great shock to Megan, as she had assumed that she would be able to live on at the farm. Her grandmother had left her a cheque for the cost of her funeral and a small sum of money for her. She also told her to contact the landlord, Mr Pritchard at the neighbouring farm. She enclosed a long letter addressed to him and asked Megan to give it to him personally.

A few days later, Megan made her way to the next farm to hand over the letter. This farm was just beautiful. To Megan it was very modern, and she loved it because there were some beautiful horses too. Mr Pritchard was a middle-aged gentleman with a very kind face. He smiled at Megan and asked if she would like to come in and have a cold glass of lemonade, as it was a very hot day. Megan accepted the drink and went into the kitchen. It was a beautiful country kitchen and so lovely and cool, even though the Aga was still on. It was a very welcoming home.

Just then, a dog came in. It was a Cavalier King Charles spaniel called Flossie, and it quickly made friends with Megan. Mr Pritchard told her Flossie was expecting puppies.

On reading the letter, Mr Pritchard suddenly gasped out loud. He looked at Megan and asked her if she knew what was in it. She said she did not, and showed him the letter her grandmother had written to her. Mr Pritchard read it and looked at her. "Well Megan, according to your grandmother, I am your father!" he said.

Megan was speechless. Could this really be true? She didn't know what shocked her more, the fact that he was her father or the fact that he had just called her Megan and not Boy, which she had become so used to being called by her family.

Mr Pritchard seemed to be in shock. He said he

had not even known that Megan's mother was pregnant. He asked her if she would mind having a DNA test done, just so that they would both be sure, and Megan agreed. She finished her lemonade and walked back home, her mind racing over the news she had just heard.

A few weeks went by and Megan heard nothing. She was desperately hoping that it was true and Mr Pritchard really was her father. Then one day there was a knock on the door and she opened it to see him standing there. He came in and told her that the test results had confirmed that he was indeed her father. After a long talk, with tears and hugs, he asked Megan if she would like to come and live with him on his farm. He had never married and had no other children. Megan was very excited, and said she was happy to move in that very afternoon.

She was given the most beautiful bedroom she could imagine. She loved the farm, and she also loved the idea that she was not expected to spend all her days working on it, because he had plenty of staff to run it for him. He was very rich and he owned nearly all the surrounding farms and land. He was very upset at how Megan had been treated.

Then Mr Pritchard asked if she would like to

learn how to ride. Megan was delighted, as she loved horses. He also said she could have a private tutor, so that she could catch up on all her studies and be at the same level as the other pupils before attending the local school. Megan agreed and soon settled down to home schooling.

When Flossie's puppies were born, Megan loved looking after them. She also loved grooming the horses, especially the new pony which her father gave her to welcome her to his home. She decided to call him Prince. Her father told her she was a natural rider. He also told her that it was important that she should learn about farming and, most importantly, how to run and manage the farms, because one day they would all be hers. Megan was overcome with sheer exuberance. She had never been so happy in her life before.

Her father was the loveliest, most caring man you could ever wish to have. He adored Megan, and Megan adored him. They had a great life together on the farm and Megan prayed every night that her father would stay healthy and live a very long life because she never wanted to lose him again.

Her only wish now was that she had known about her father all those years ago. She also felt a great sadness that her mother had not married her father, because they would have had such a wonderful life together and her mother would have been so happy. She also realised that the important thing now was for her to enjoy her lovely new home and not take what she had for granted.

She had grown up into a lovely young lady and had made some nice friends at the local school. She realised how fortunate she was and what a good thing it was that her grandparents had taken her in all those years ago, although she had not fully appreciated this at the time. She loved being treated like the princesses she had read about in many of her fairy-tale stories. For Megan her dreams had come true. She had now finally found her happy ever after.

# THE WHITE WICKER CHAIR

Hilda smiled to herself. She had recently been admitted temporarily to a hospital ward, as she had fallen and had badly sprained her ankle. She was grateful that she was allowed to bring in her small wicker chair into hospital with her, together with her jewellery box and her own clothes to wear, instead of the awful hospital gowns. She loved her wicker chair. It was very comfortable and had beautifully soft cushions.

Little did the staff know just how important that wicker chair was, because the cushions held a secret, a secret that only Hilda knew. When you have a secret, it gives you power, and she intended to use that power one day. She did not know when the right time would come, but she felt happy to know that one day it would all be revealed.

The dilemma she faced now was whether she should reveal her secret while she was alive or leave it to be found in her will. The secret gave her comfort, especially when she was alone for hours in her room with nothing to do except look out of her window or watch the television. The staff saw her as a kind old lady, polite and intelligent for 70. Hilda could not believe that she had managed to keep her secrets for over 20 years, for her secret was that she had committed murder – and not just once.

Hilda was a great cook, and everyone enjoyed her cakes. Little did they know that if anyone upset her she would pop around to their house and offer them one of her special cupcakes. They were special because they contained poison, of a kind which could not be detected during a post mortem. It was a drug which acted slowly, usually taking about 24 hours, and left no trace.

Hilda always insisted that whether they were in their house or in Hilda's, the person having the cake should eat it with her over a cup of tea, so she could make sure that the person she intended to kill took the poison and not an innocent person. The poison would not normally work until the following day, so Hilda knew that no one would suspect that she was the culprit. If she visited the house with the intended poison, she made sure that the dishes were washed before she left. She would offer to do them, but the host always declined and did them first. Hilda then took the plastic box back home, so that no one would know that she had even visited. She always wore white lace cotton gloves, explaining that she had dry, sore hands, and that became the reason why the host always washed up while Hilda was there so that she would not get her hands wet. That way, there were no fingerprints on any of the surfaces she touched. Of course most of the murders were committed in Hilda's own home, so that when the person left, she could easily get rid of all the evidence.

All was going well, until one day Hilda had a fall and ended up in hospital, which meant that she was unable to complete her next murder.

Hilda's first murder had been arranged 20 years before, when she had worked as a secretary in a solicitor's office in the nearby town. Hilda was single. She never married and was an only child, so when her parents died, she stayed on at the large Victorian family home her parents had left to her and where she hoped one day to have her own family. She started working as a secretary to a solicitor called Mr Armstrong. Eventually, after she had been working for him for some years, they had an affair. Hilda fell madly in love with him, but he, sadly, did not fall in love with her. One day Mr Armstrong called her into his office and told her he was ending their relationship. He said that he was going to employ a new secretary, and that he would give Hilda three months' salary if she left immediately. What made it worse was that it happened to be Hilda's 50th birthday. She was devastated, especially when the next day she went back to collect her things from her desk and walked in to find Mr Armstrong kissing the new secretary. She was furious, especially as she knew that the girl was married.

One day while Hilda was at home, she decided to try her hand at baking. She found an old recipe book of her mother's and started to bake cakes, and she soon became very good at it. Baking also helped to pass the time. It was during this time while she was cooking that she thought about how she could get revenge on Mr Armstrong. After all, they had been in a relationship for a very long time, and secretly Hilda had felt sure they would get married one day, but it had all been a lie.

Then an idea came to her. Maybe she could find a poison that could not be tasted in a cake. She knew just how much he loved cakes. After lots of research at the library she found a natural substance that could be used, and she managed to get all she needed from a shop in a nearby town. So one Friday afternoon she took her cake, baked with her new "recipe", into the office. She explained that she was very sorry for being upset when she was last there, and said it was just the shock at having to leave her employment so abruptly. She said she wanted to remain friends and to show that there were no hard feelings she wanted to make a peace offering. Then she handed them the cake she had made, saying it was for Mr Armstrong and his new secretary to share. Of course they were stupid people, in Hilda's eyes, to believe such a story, but believe it they did. They both ate some cake, and within 24 hours they were both dead.

The following day, knowing that the office would be empty, Hilda used her key to gain access and started on her next plan. She knew her boss kept his will in his office safe, and of course Hilda knew the combination. She was delighted that he had not yet changed the code.

She opened the safe and very carefully read the will. She noted that she had been left £1,000 for long service to the company. Hilda knew that her boss had no family. Carefully she changed the 1 to a 7, making her share £7,000. She then put the amended will back into the safe. A few months later she received a cheque for £7,000 from Mr Armstrong's estate. She was delighted that her plan had worked.

After this incident, Hilda went on to kill many more women. Because the poison was not detectable, the cause of death went down as natural causes or causes unknown. For the next 20 years, Hilda kept a record of the date and name of everyone she had killed in a small book sewn into her cushion. She also had a small packet of the poison sewn inside another cushion, which she kept in her white wicker chair. Over the years, she changed her personality into a frail little old lady who was just a good listener. No one really noticed her, but everyone came to eat her cakes and tell her their stories.

No one was ever interested in Hilda's life, only their own. Hilda thought this was very selfish and she felt that what she was doing was a good thing because she was getting rid of horrible deceitful people. After all, if they were stupid enough to talk to her about their affairs, their abortions and so on, then they should be punished. And it was her job to make sure they were.

She always visited the ones who lived alone on a Friday afternoon so that they would not be discovered until either they had not returned to work on the Monday or the milk or post had piled up and the neighbours noticed that the person had not been seen for a few days. The weekend gave the poison time to break down, if it was not disturbed for 48 hours, so it could not be detected. Then she would just sit and wait for someone to come and tell her the terrible news. She was quite the agony aunt of the village. Women of all ages visited her, bringing local gossip.

Hilda insisted on her chair coming with her into hospital because she didn't want anyone finding it at her house, as she was going to be in for eight weeks. Every night before she went to sleep she reached for her chair, dug out her book and wrote down the names of the staff who had confided their dirty secrets to her that day. After leaving hospital she would be inviting certain people to come for tea with her as a thank you.

Eventually Hilda returned home. Her leg was still painful, but she was able to walk with the help of a stick. Upon arriving home, she was surprised to find that she had very little post to open, only a handful of get well cards. She was disappointed that not many of her "friends" had visited her in hospital or had missed her after she had spent hours listening to all their stories. She decided to ring them all and let them know that she was now at home and that they could visit her at any time.

A few days later her visitors started to arrive. Only a few of them were really interested in how Hilda felt, so she decided that she would take revenge on the visitors who were not interested in her with a new plan. This involved getting the cakes to the offending staff at the hospital, as she was unable to walk properly yet.

There were four of them in particular who had offended her. She gave these visitors, who were not very nice people, in Hilda's opinion, the names of the nurses who had confided to Hilda that they were in relationships with other women's men. She gave each of the four one person to contact per month, and instructed them all to invite these people to tea with Hilda and to come along themselves.

The first date was arranged and the first visitor proudly came with the nurse. They both shared the delicious cakes Hilda had made, and they were both dead 24 hours later. The same thing happened with the other three, so within in a space of four months, eight people had been killed by Hilda's deadly cakes and no one had any idea of her involvement.

Hilda was very pleased that she had accomplished her mission to get rid of some of the cheating and unkind people in the village and nearby towns. She had no sense of guilt whatsoever. As far as she was concerned she was doing the community a favour by getting rid of these awful women. Hilda put the names of the last eight victims in her secret diary and placed it back inside the cushion in her chair.

A week after the last murder had taken place, Hilda decided that it was time to start spending the money she had acquired from her boss, and maybe have a holiday. The next day she got ready and left to go to the bank. She decided that she would put her diary into a safe deposit safe at the bank for safe keeping. She drew out a large sum of money, and after some lunch in town she went shopping and bought several new dresses, jackets and even two evening dresses in bright colours. She also found some very nice pairs of shoes. It was a very pleasant experience for Hilda to shop for clothes, as she had been wearing the same "old ladies' outfits" in black or grey for the last few years.

She took a taxi home with her purchases and put her new clothes away in her wardrobe. As she was having a cup of tea she saw an advert in the paper about a world cruise. This, thought Hilda, was just what she needed. It was time for her to stop all the murders and enjoy some fun and spend some money.

She rang the telephone number in the paper and asked for more details. After talking to a very pleasant sales girl for some time, she booked herself on a cruise to the Mediterranean. For the first time in many years, Hilda was excited. She was to leave in two weeks' time.

That evening Hilda walked to the local postbox and sent off her cheque for the cruise. All she needed to do now was wait for her itinerary and tickets to arrive. She spent the next few days shopping and packing her suitcase with all the lovely new clothes she had bought. She did not want her visitors to know that she was going on a cruise, so she told them she was going to visit her sister who lived in London. No one questioned her about her sister. They just wished her a pleasant journey and started to wonder where they would be able to get decent cakes while she was away. Typical, thought Hilda. They were not coming to visit me. They just came for my free cakes!

After her visitors had left, Hilda polished and

cleaned her house. It was gleaming and smelt of lavender polish. She vacuumed the floors, and finally she got rid of the last sachet of poison down the toilet. She still had a small amount left in her chair. She then sat down to a cup of tea and fell asleep in her wicker chair.

She awoke to sound of the doorbell, which startled her. Who on earth would be calling at this hour? She glanced at the clock. It was 6 pm, which was late for any of her visitors. When she opened the door, she was shocked to see two police officers on the doorstep. She invited them in and they explained why they had come to see her. The senior officer, who introduced himself as Detective Inspector Wyles, said he wanted to ask her questions about one of her friends, a Miss Aldridge (this was the last visitor Hilda had murdered), to see if she knew anything that could help with their inquiry. The officer said Miss Aldridge had written in her diary that she was having tea with Hilda on the Friday before she was found dead, and he wondered if she had said anything to Hilda about her health, as the coroner had found an abnormality during the post mortem.

This really shocked Hilda. She was very flustered, but she managed to cover this by pretending to shed a tear for the late Miss Aldridge. The news was so very distressing for her, she told the officer. She said that Miss Aldridge had been in terrible pain with arthritis (which Hilda remembered was true).

"Do you think that maybe the pain got so bad that the poor dear got confused and took too many painkillers by mistake, and that caused the abnormality?" Hilda asked Detective Inspector Wyles. He replied, "It is possible she got confused. We'll know more next week after they have finished the tests after the post mortem." At this point he took his leave and thanked Hilda for her help, saying he would let her know the outcome. Hilda quickly said that she was going away in a few days to visit her sick sister, but that she would look forward to hearing about her poor friend when she returned.

The officers said goodbye and promised to be in touch. After they had left, Hilda was physically sick. What if they looked into the other deaths? And what if other victims had kept diaries? What if they had mentioned they had visited Hilda, or she had visited them?

Her mind was in a turmoil. It had never occurred to her that anyone would write the details of the visits in a diary or discuss them with anyone. She became very agitated and afraid at this thought. One thing Hilda knew now was that she would never have the courage to confess her crimes, and she did not want to go to prison. She had to think of a way to escape and not get caught. She had three days before her cruise to try and decide what to do.

Then she remembered Ronnie, and a plan started to form in her mind. She had met him at Mr Armstrong's office when he was doing some work for him. Ronnie was an expert in checking for forgeries, and he had been known to alter legal documents, if the price was right. Hilda had learnt a lot from Ronnie, including how to alter a will undetected.

She rang Ronnie and arranged to meet him at a coffee house in town the next morning. When he arrived, she asked him if he could possibly help her to get a passport done for her twin sister. She said that her sister had been ill and it was Hilda's wish to take her on holiday before she died. The problem was that she did not have a passport and was not expected to live for too long, so there was no time to wait to get a new passport issued.

Ronnie said it was possible, but it would cost a lot of money. Hilda assured him that the cost did not worry her. He said he would need a photograph. Hilda had expected this, so she was prepared and gave him an old photograph of herself taken five years ago. She said they were identical twins, and the only difference between them was that her sister had blonde hair, so could he use this photograph? Ronnie said it would take him a few hours, but he was confident that he would have the passport ready for collection the following day. He asked her what her sister's name was and Hilda said it was Rosie Maye.

Hilda left the shop after agreeing to meet Ronnie the next day at 10am with the money. She was very relieved that she would now have a new identity and passport.

The following day Hilda met with Ronnie and they exchanged the passport for the money, in cash over another cup of coffee. Hilda was happy with the passport, and she gave Ronnie a homemade cupcake she had made. She asked him if he would like to have it with another cup of coffee, to which he agreed. After he had eaten his cake and finished his coffee, they said goodbye. Hilda did feel very bad that she had to kill Ronnie with the very last dose of the poison she had sewn into her chair, but it would ruin her plan if he told the police about the fake passport. She needed the police to think she was still in London visiting her sister.

When she returned home she booked a taxi for 9 am the next day to take her to Victoria Coach Station, where she would catch the coach to Southampton.

Then she cleaned her home and put all the cake ingredients and tins, including all her rubbish, outside for the dustman to collect the next day. She arranged for her phone to be disconnected, and then she walked to the post box with the cheques for her bills, including a letter requesting that the electricity be cut off as she was going to visit her sister in London for a few weeks. She then lit her fire and burned all the paperwork of her life. She then packed her old ladies' clothes into another holdall, ready with her suitcase.

As she drove away in the taxi the next morning she knew with sadness that she would not be returning to her home again. On the way she stopped at the local cemetery where her parents were buried. She left a beautiful bunch of flowers with a card saying "RIP from your loving daughter Hilda x" That evening she set sail from Southampton docks for her round-the-world cruise.

Hilda really enjoyed her cruise. She loved the food, the drinks and the wonderful entertainment every evening. After a few weeks they finally arrived in Sydney. This was to be the last stage of Hilda's plan, and the end of "Hilda" herself.

When the ship docked at Sydney, all passengers were asked to leave their suitcases outside their cabins, where they would be collected by the cruise staff and transferred onto another ship for the next part of their cruise. Hilda packed all her old ladies' clothes into the big suitcase along with her evening dresses and packed her new clothes into the holdall. She then left the large suitcase outside her cabin and headed through customs as Hilda for the very last time.

She was supposed to go on a coach trip around Sydney, but she informed the guide that she had decided not to go and that she would prefer to stay behind and board the next ship later. The guide was happy with this, as it was one less old lady for him to be concerned with, and there were already a very large number of people queuing for the coach. Hilda went into the ladies' toilets and was pleased to see when she came out that the coach had left.

She then went for a walk around the shops, feeling pleased that so far her plan was working. She managed to find a hairdresser who could fit her in right away. She had her hair dyed and styled just like her new passport photograph. The assistant did a wonderful job and Hilda looked much younger, being blonde rather than grey. She took a taxi to Sydney

Airport, where she changed into a new outfit and left her old clothes in a bin. She boarded the plane for New Zealand as Rosie Maye and then got a taxi to the hotel she had previously booked.

After staying at the hotel for two weeks and getting used to her new identity as Rosie, she started to look for an apartment to rent. She found a delightful one-bedroom apartment which was fully furnished. She paid two years' rent in advance with the remainder of her money.

The apartment was in a very small cul-de-sac with other people of similar ages. Rosie was accepted into the very small community and for the first time seemed to be accepted for herself. When she was asked one day if she could bake cakes Rosie replied "No, I have never been much of a baker," but she did show an interest in gardening, and one or two people were happy to invite her to come and see their gardens. They also invited her to join them to play cards once a month at the local town hall.

For the first time in a very long time Rosie was happy. She really enjoyed her new friends' company and she was very pleased that they were kind people and not gossipers.

Time passed, and Rosie realised that each day she was getting older and more frail, and her breathing was getting more difficult. She decided she really ought to make arrangements for her funeral. She made an appointment with the local funeral director, who showed her various options. She explained that she had no family but that she would like to be cremated, and for her ashes to be scattered at sea. She then paid in full for all her funeral costs.

The next job was to go to a local solicitor and arrange to have a will drawn up. She asked the solicitor to keep a letter in his safe and said it was to be posted in Sydney, Australia after her death. She gave him money for his return flight and extra cash for him to carry out her wishes.

The letter was to Detective Inspector Wyles, and in it she confessed to the murders she had committed. She also included the key to her safe deposit box for him to open at her bank in England. Inside the box was her little book with the list of dates and names in and the reason they had all had to die (all except Ronnie's details - she did not mention that murder).

She wanted to be remembered by her new friends in New Zealand for being a nice person, rather than an old lady who listened to gossip and murdered people. She felt it would be better if the letter was posted in Australia, in case the detective ever decided to try and find her. If that happened, the trail of Hilda would end in Australia, and he would not know of the existence of Rosie Maye in New Zealand.

Rosie continued to live a secluded but happy life. She enjoyed her time in New Zealand and loved the views. The highlight of each evening was looking at all the photographs she had taken of her cruise and remembering all the beautiful countries she had visited.

After her death, her ashes were scattered at sea. Her few possessions were given to local friends, and the little money that was left was given to a local charity.

Rosie's letter was duly posted in Sydney, Australia to the detective in England by her solicitor as requested. Along with her confession, Hilda said that her large Victorian house in England was to be used as a refuge for vulnerable women who had been hurt either physically or mentally by their husbands or boyfriends, because she herself had never really recovered from the pain of the breakup of her relationship, or from not being able to have the children she had wanted. It was this hurt that had led her down the path of murdering women who had confided in her that they had cheated on their partners or had abortions. Hilda wanted the women who had been left with broken hearts to be cared for in the family home where she had felt so safe.

She also requested that her white wicker chair with the lovely comfortable cushions should go to the local cat sanctuary for the cats there to sleep on.

When Detective Inspector Wyles read Hilda's letter and retrieved her diary from the safe deposit box, he was astounded to read that she had committed 14 murders. Although he was shocked to read all about the crimes, and her reasons for committing them, what shocked him most was that he had had no idea about her secret. To him she had been just a lovely little old lady who happened to be rather good at baking.